I0713252

Seven Stories

Seven Stories

Leo Birch

Full Court Press
Englewood Cliffs, New Jersey

Published in the United States of America
by Full Court Press, 601 Palisade Avenue,
Englewood Cliffs, NJ 07632
fullcourtpress.com

PRINT ISBN 978-1-953728-31-9
EBOOK ISBN 978-1-953728-35-7
Library of Congress Control No. 2024906669

Editing and book design by Barry Sheinkopf

CHEERS TO LIFE

CHEERS TO LIFE

Table of Contents

ACQUA ALTA

T HE ELEVATED PATHWAYS WERE UP. The rain seemed to be everywhere. In the *lagune*, the sky, and everything in between, you could only see sheets of liquid gray.

Those wooden elevated pathways allowed pedestrians to walk over the lowest point of the city when the canals swelled high enough to submerge the stones of the streets, and the water reached above the last step of the Venetian stairways: magical stairways that seemed to lead straight down into unknown depths.

A city of mysteries and mistresses.

A city always waiting for the next flood, as unavoidable as age itself.

They strolled along the narrow streets, stepping cautiously over the wet stones as they walked through the city, meandering along streets where there was only room for rain.

He closed the umbrella. It had just become too wide for the walls. They sought refuge in a small trattoria for lunch. The pasta came steaming hot and *al dente*, and with it the requisite glass of wine. "A glass of red," he'd said, and it appeared at the discretion of the waiter. There was no fancy review of a list or such; it was an unspoken act of trust—*I sit down at your table, in your restaurant, and you will take care of us.* A simple transaction, yet seemingly so perverted in the world they had come from.

Her laughter resonated in the room like flowers.

Their bodies warmed by the food and wine, they finally decided to go back outside. Large pools of rainwater had accumulated on the path back to the Palazzo Hotel, and they could not avoid them all. So it was with wet shoes in hand and laughing out loud that they rushed into the luxury of their suite. The rain beating down on the windowpanes that faced the majestic Grand Canal sounded like distant drums that almost magically merged seamlessly with the vintage jazz music already filling the room.

The bed had been done, a willing hand neatly straightening out the last wrinkle before the maid left. It looked like a wrapped gift.

And she took it.

Slipping her still cold frame in the folds of whiteness—shivering from the pleasure of anticipation of his warm body, opening up to allow him to completely heat her up.

She nestled against it—tightly.

Skin to skin.

He was significantly older than she was, the kind of man who still carried a cotton handkerchief in his pocket. And she said she loved it. She loved his age, his way in life, and especially his way when he touched her and found her.

By the canal, the gradient of the moss on the stairway steps outlined the passage of time.

2

HIS LEG BETWEEN HERS, she soaked in all the heat that his pressure could transmit—her own hands wrapped around him, fingers lingering on his thick neck.

She drank from his chest with the silvery hair, absorbing the nascent heat, shifting herself to fit even tighter against him.

She liked him tight against her.

Heavy on her.

His weight, her refuge.

She pulled him in even closer, feeling how big he had become in that short moment between a warm casual embrace and the luscious wave of desire that flowed now between them. Her hand played with him, caressing it lovingly, as you would a sculpture, after hours, in a closed museum. Outside did not matter any longer. There was nothing else but the contained world of their bed. That, and the erotic imagery he spoke softly in her ear, his words like lava.

She did not always wish to go with the flow of his decadence, but the sound of his voice made it all happen. A voice that mesmerized her into wanting more and saying "yes" to anything he said just to listen to it some more. Her eyes fluttered, as if to listen harder, and she felt him slip in and out of her.

Outside, waves rhythmically lapped the top steps of the stairs in the lagune.

He was hard enough to lift her light frame up from the bed. Instead, his arm wrapped itself around her thigh and held on hard to her ass.

3

SHE WAS PINNED.

She was taken.

The bed height was perfect for him, and he took her to the edge. The light that streamed through the hotel windows was blue and vivid, while the bedside table lamps glowed soft and golden on their skin.

And always, behind the hotel walls, the waters were flowing fast in the canals.

She looked at the screen of the phone camera as he pointed it towards her. Watched him take her slowly, his anatomy in full view one moment, and then disappearing in her as by magic—at a pace of his own, as if traveling along a story that unfolded as he saw fit.

His long fingers feeling her.

At first, it was the softest of touches, freeing the tools of her imagination. And then, she heard them coming loud and crisp in the immaculate air, every slap tingling her naked skin with a delicious burn that caused her entire body to shiver.

She was loving every bit of it, succumbing so completely to the fervor of such pleasure that time ceased to exist.

History itself got sucked out from the narrow Venetian gateways.

Only in the void that followed did she eventually drift back slowly to herself, unaware of everything she had acquiesced to, of promises made. Her face was still lost in the pillows.

Gradually, the words resonated back to her like an echo through distant palatial rooms, filling her with images of the decadence he suggested. She had been presented with a challenge. A task for her to accept. And with that, waters were rising within her, passionate, solid, forceful.

She was of two minds—there was no other man but him. Her love.

Her lover.

All encompassing.

And yet there was a seriousness to his request. His tone had always been demanding as he hovered over her, day after day, and into the nights, time and time again. She had wondered if he really meant it, but after what he now said at the hotel, she knew he did.

He told her to follow her own inner impulses, the ones that had pushed her already to seduce—to flirt, to feel the glances over her body, her neck, her skin— to follow her inner nature.

The next day, the water had reached the high-level mark.

4

SHE TOOK HER SHOES OFF AS SHE CROSSED the piazza, a square opening of light and space and life within the city's maze. Strangely enough she felt like a free bird crossing the last street just as it started to overflow. Ever so soon after that, she took her clothes off in front of the stranger.

She saw her reflection in an elegant, ancient mirror, and she liked what she saw—the black garters and her flesh blending gracefully within the old shadow of the glass and its history of past glimpses.

Her legs uncrossed as she sat on the table. His head lodged beneath her, his thick, dark hair brushing against her warm skin. His tongue reached her here and there. He was between her. He was starving for her. And she felt each foreign sensation—every stroke, lick, and touch. Feeling but not fully realizing what was happening.

Was she really doing this?

Was it actually, really happening?

Or was her lover making it happen from afar, as if close to her—as if he was the one who placed the camera phone in her hands and made her take the picture of her open legs, as if he was the one who also pressed *Send.*

Outside, a delicate bird flew by, close enough to almost crash through the room's large panel windows as if destined to plunge through the ancient glass.

It flew by unscathed, though, and disappeared into the gray sky. She was the only one to witness that.

She *knew* it was actually happening. She could feel it. She could feel the curls of this stranger, a man she had met only hours before, rubbing against the inside of her thighs. She held onto the edge of the wooden ledge of that solid tabletop. A good writing desk, she thought, pressing her palms against the dark walnut as she pushed herself forward on his face, feeding herself to him as she embraced him between her legs. She smiled at the thought of a future guest sitting at the desk she was rubbing against. She watched his shoulders move in unison with her waist, his hands wrapped around her legs. She wanted him to lift her up, to forcefully take her on the desk or swing her onto the bed. She thought about what she wanted him to do for her, and she suddenly noticed it.

She was aware of him, of everything.

Of his moves.

Of his youth.

Of his dependence to her own moves.

Her lips curved up in a quiet smile at the realization of how things unfolded differently with her lover. How he took control for both of them, and took her in order for her to get lost in a forest of repeated pleasures and a ground so soft that they floated in it.

The waters were rising.

Outside there was the gentle thud of banging wood as the moving gondolas connected with their high hung moorings.

Oh, how much she would like for this man to link her arms above her head, as her lover did, and possess her! But this, she realized, was not to happen. She was here on a mission, she reminded herself. A sacrificial act of tenderness for her own man.

She pushed herself onto him, forcing him to sit on the desk chair. And then, legs apart, she sat on him. She took his whole length in her body, engulfing him entirely, moving purposefully with the slow burn of the relentless fervor of a task to be done, fully lucid of her present role. Then a moan slipped through her lips.

"Like a high-class whore," he had told her.

And she played the part well. She had chosen black lace stockings showing off the top of her legs. That space of skin had driven the man on the chair insanely crazy when he mustered the courage to reach under her partly raised skirt at the after-dinner club party a short while before. His hand was an island in the midst of the throngs of revelers in the dark palazzo room. He was convinced that the music pulsing from the DJ table had urged him to do it, unaware that, actually, she was the one willing him to.

Outside the party, the phantoms of boats returning victorious from battle glided unnoticed on the canals, below the suspended balconies.

Tall, most likely Italian, wealthy in watch and clothes, she had immediately picked him out in the crowd and let him get closer and closer. Mesmerized, he had danced with her, for her, getting closer as the mass of people grew thicker on the dance floor.

The beat of the dance music had blanketed the swaying bodies, hiding the fading frescos on the once-glorious ceiling of the palazzo hall. As the dancing went on, his hand touched hers. She'd smiled. He had danced harder, his eyes focused on her in the darkness, her hips hallucinating.

She'd thought about it for a moment. She was going to do this after all.

He had been asking for it, over and over.

She'd felt her body swing into action, as if trained by his words, his voice clear in her mind, and leaned forward and asked him to take her to a quieter place.

And then later that same evening, she had pressed *Send*.

In a distant room, his phone buzzed signaling a new message. His eyes widened as he opened the image. It was incredibly powerful, and it burned through the digital screen and pierced the space between his eyes, burrowing itself deep into the most primal part of his brain, bouncing on the walls of his thoughts and desires and propelling him to the room where she was doing it all for him.

There was no doubt about the image. Even the blurriness of the photo suggested the reality of that moment, her hand shaking a little as she took the shot. He could imagine her hands now, climbing along the width of the man's chest and body, reaching him, pulling him. And her mouth deep on his throb as she emptied him on her lips, her mouth, her face.

She left the Italian man exhausted and spent, still panting on the chair as she dutifully went to the bathroom to take one last picture. Walking out, she looked at him again as he now lay asleep on his unmade bed. His limbs long and thin. His chest narrow and elegant. His eyes closed, face reflecting utter and incomprehensible ecstasy. She watched his breath steadily rise and meet the same point and, satisfied, she turned away and left. She knew she would never see him again.

6

HER HIPS STILL FLUSHED WITH SEX, she walked back through Venice to their hotel room.

She missed the flesh of her own man, the weight of his strong arms around her, his chest a trunk. She loved that he stayed with her even after they were both spent, and wet, and done, in a flow of thoughts and voids. She loved how he could reawaken her still pulsing flesh.

Over the stones, the water kept rising.

People had to use those elevated pathways now, the noise of their steps drumming along the walls of the citadels. The moss marking the usual high-water line was visible only at times, when the waves crawled away from the solid facades, revealing that thin layer of moss, a demarcation between the usual tides and the overflow, between the normal and the immortal.

Watered streets, overfilled now with energy, flowed all throughout the delicate architectural city like veins along a living body, a breathing being exhaling endlessly.

All she wanted now was to go back to her lover. . .

Go back to him and feel the full expenditure of his being, of his flesh.

He was the *acqua alta*—the man among the boys. And she wanted him crushing her under his body.

She raced the rest of the way, eager to enter the magnificent lobby of the old hotel and recapture her reflection in the smoked mirrors of the decadent private elevator. She flew out of it and sped to the room, high above the waterline.

Rain streamed at a steady pace. The windowpanes had become studded with water drops, each reflecting the night lights in its own particular way.

There were no lights on in the room. She had hoped for him to be waiting up here, maybe with a glass in hand and a smile on his face. The room, even with all its luxuries, appeared empty without him.

She paused as she turned around to reach for the lights and reflected upon what she had just done for him. For his love, his wish, his desire. And yet, also, she reflected, for herself. Not the sex really, but the picking-up part. Yes, the seduction game. And after the seduction, being able to let it all unfold as if by fate: new hands, new feelings, new experience, and by being detached, allowing herself to focus on him a little longer, almost clinically, and thus play with him. But right now, what she wanted more than anything was validation of her role, like a schoolgirl waiting for an accolade for a job well done.

The lavender sofa was caught in the limelight of the room. Everything suddenly seemed too bright. She dimmed the ceiling light and kept only the small table lamps on; their halo duplicated in the dark windows, lighting up the cascading raindrops.

She felt unsure of herself. She wondered, *Did I go too far?* It'd all happened so fast at the end, as if she had tumbled in a sea of waves.

She put on a jazz compilation that he had made for her; it started with Coltrane, and it was perfect. She sat down on the sofa, skirt off, stockings off, resting on a small towel she had placed earlier, her inner thighs still tingling. Her mind drifted away for a short while. She felt lost by now.

She stood up and was about to reach for a grape from the sumptuous fruit basket resting on the credenza when she decided she wanted to shower instead. Or maybe even take a bath today?

She felt it before she saw it. There was someone moving behind her. It came from the bedroom. She felt the stir of the air. Her body tensed at once— legs, limbs all tight.

She tilted her head slightly and from the corner of her eye she saw the shape.

7

ON THE WAY BACK TO THE HOTEL she had stopped by Claudio's antique store. Maybe it was the rain that had suddenly amplified a desire, or a need to see something beautiful after what she had just done. She'd walked in the store almost mechanically, as if weighted down by a wave of doubt that had suddenly manifested itself—le vague à l'âme, the French would call it.

She wondered about everything—how she was leading her life, what her future would be.

Was it useless, being in love with such an older man and loving that, too?

Was she destined to reach that cliff and have all the water pour down at once, a long waterfall cascading down the slope of her hopes and perhaps hubris?

"But I do love him," she whispered to herself.

Like no one else before. And maybe never after.

And she had always led her life according to her love, following the instinctual path of her emotions, seeing them flickering like petals in the wind.

Was that solid ground enough to make it all happen?

Could she live thinking only of the now? Of that elusive moment that her age brought with her?

She entered the narrow store through the side door, leaving the wet and even more narrow streets behind her. Her transparent white raincoat dripped translucent on the storefront carpet. Beautiful glass vases and cups lined the upper shelves. Within their core the glass objects contained the green of spring leaves and the yellow of flowers in the sun. Swirls of color mixed with bubbles of air blown into the liquid glass, like souls into men. She let her eyes wander on these shapes, mesmerized by the transparence of them, bemused by the delicate fragility. They were so much like her, she thought.

In perfect Italian, she spoke softly to the shopkeeper. The woman wore her glasses on the tip of her nose as she leafed through index cards to find the prices, words flowing from her as if they were butterflies in the glass shop. They seemed to be the only two living people in Venice at that instant.

Outside , the thick drops resonated on the floor stones and the store-front window. She felt as if she were floating in an aquatic palace, submerged in glass and light. She walked away with the pale green vase they had both looked at together earlier in the trip. It was to be a surprise. Just as her picture with semen running through her lips had been a surprise.

8

SHE TURNED AROUND AND FACED the presence she had felt and was bewildered to see him. It was him. There was no doubt about it. And he was smiling at her—the good-looking Italian man she had just seduced in so many ways just earlier in the night.

And from the shadows of the other bedroom, she saw her own man emerge. Like a director slowly coming onstage. A magician of sorts.

When she saw him, she relaxed and waited as he dimmed the lights even further and, before she could muster a word, she felt the hands. Two of them at first, climbing along the stem of her legs. And two more hands, his, this time, powerfully resting on her neck and throat like a necklace of lust. Her head tilted back, she met his cock and took it.

She took him while he was still small and she could fit it all in her mouth, loving it as it grew bigger and larger and almost exploded out of her, the flesh growing within her lips until she could fit only the tip. She tasted every inch of him and let her smile run smoothly along the hard cylinder.

A flood of new sensations overtook her as she felt them both on her. She could feel her body being toyed with; it was overwhelming at first but slowly, willingly, she let herself join the dance, her movements eventually seeking theirs.

Her hip thrust high onto the manhood and down again, as if breathing in the tide of the *lagunes*, the swells of the canal, and the liquid fury of the rainy storm.

Up along their shafts as if they were masts on boats in a tempest, offering all of herself in carnal delight, her frame light and malleable.

Hands floated her up, lifting her upon tables and sofa tops, and through the soft fabric of the seductive sheets.

Legs apart. Ass spread. And her mouth always open, thirsty for more.

On the canal, swollen waves kept raising the wooden gondolas, built with hollow cockpits shaped like the intimacy of a woman, and the two bows arched and curved like solid manhood.

Then the stranger left.

And it was just the two of them again.

9

SHE SLEPT IN A DEEP SLUMBER, moaning at times in the depth of her dreams, as if in the body of a whale, unaware.

Outside, the rising water overflowed the highest watermark ever.

Some revelers were still out, escaping the rain in cavernous party rooms; wide indulgent spaces reverberating with soft music with champagne glasses filled to the hilt, foam slipping out above the rims. The city itself seemed quieter, noise dampened by the deep hum of the falling rain.

The next morning, as soon as she woke up, she looked for

him and was satisfied only when she saw him writing at the mahogany desk, his hand reaching out for grapes from time to time.

Something had changed, and she could not quite grasp what it was exactly.

She let herself fall back on the soft pillows, her long hair an aura along her face. Again, she thought and searched. Last night's events hardly registered, gone as if they had never happened, the decadent fantasies swept away by the morning light, leaving her alone with her love for her man.

She remained still for a while, resisting the urge to put on her long purple silk gown and go to him. She laid still until she finally realized what had so drastically changed—the rain had stopped. The windows were quiet again, the boats finally silent.

Her robe opened as she leaned forward, arching towards his face. Her eyes were still half-closed from the brighter light of the room and her smile still full of sex. Her naked body catching the morning haze begged him to come back to bed with her. They walked through the deep mantle of the bedroom entrance as if in a temple, and he lay down next to her heat and laziness, bodies linked in horizontal bliss and in total abandon, far from stories and tales.

He was her high watermark.

They rested, breathing in the centuries, as time slowed down just a bit—breathing in the costumes, and the treasures and the treasons, the grandeur of the floating city and all its structures that seemed to move when the waters flowed.

Soon enough, his manhood turned into a spire, a column of desire, almost as if it had to be, even if he was content to just linger. It grew between them, and she felt it—a separate animal that longed for her, and how its curved crown somehow beautifully matched her inlet. There was no saliva needed.

The top sheet went up and covered them both, hiding the incoming light and setting the tent in which they would get lost in motion. Moments later, his sweat dripped drop by drop on her willing body, her hands sliding up and down his wet torso of stone and grabbing his ass to plunge him even deeper in her, as if it were possible.

Twilight juices kept pouring out of her as he repeatedly penetrated her body and fulfilled her wishes. With the softest of touches, his long fingers found their way along her crest, and in sweat and tears of joy she let herself become liquid under him, becoming yet another river that fed the city of romantic souls.

For him.

For her.

ELEMENTAL

—I'm Ready, My Lord

F YOU DON'T RETELL A TALE, WHERE DOES IT GO? Is it worth living it? Outside, by the small natural harbor of pale gray water, ospreys are flying. They are beautiful birds of prey. They fish with their talons only.

He watched as two juveniles were attempting their first flights. A cup of dark tea in a white porcelain mug in his hand, he is back home—while she is still over there, in her vacation home on the small island of Patmos, a dot in the Mediterranean Sea.

The flights of the birds overlap for a moment. They move in unison within his field of view. From a different vantage, they would be moving apart.

The ospreys, he recalls, are the only raptors that can be

found on all five continents: a species with a ubiquitous display of adaptability and resilience.

He wages an interesting balance with her. She stays alone over there for a few weeks while he remains working back in the city. She feeds him stories, scripts, scenarios, even the occasional photo. In return, he refrains from seeking his own stories and follies. He lives on them. She knows it. She has seen it. Therefore, she constantly feeds him from the threshold of her distant isle.

It is a balance. They're like two kids on that plank toy you see in some playgrounds, pivoting around a fixed axis. One up and one down. Always linked.

One of the two juvenile ospreys has grass caught in its claws. The adult, Mom, he guesses, keeps an eye on his flight. The youth makes it back safely to the tremendous nest made of thick twigs, perched high above ground. Each early flight is an adventure. No one will ever remember it unless it is read again.

Water

FAR AWAY ON THE ISLAND, THE WATERS ARE PURE and beautiful in the bay, almost virginal. By chance, the two of them swam towards each other. Light reflects itself, not only on the surface, but also underneath it and it bathed their bodies with indolent colors. She watched his hand disappear in the water with each stroke, shoulders moving smoothly along the axis of his trunk and hips, his skin alternatively tanned and white within the greens and myriads of blues.

They saw themselves as simply swimming.

The moment had a movie-like quality, and it was as if they became even more beautiful under the fictional digital gaze. Although they were swimming towards each other it was towards a point where they actually would not meet. That would be too perfect, and cliché. They were moving and swimming because it was their destiny. And because the souls, sitting close by or in the distance, were willing them to.

ONCE YOU REACH ANOTHER DIMENSION, once you leave the third dimension in which we dwell in on this earth, you enjoy life, or existence really, through the spectrum of earthly human experiences. If you are rewarded in life, you get to thrive on the loving experiences and emotions of living human beings. You get to feel their joys and pleasures as it was for instance when you inhaled the invisible sweet perfume of a rose back on solid Earth.

They swam past each other. She did not like to put her face in the water, and this gave him more time to see her. His gaze lingered on her smiling eyes, and then he went under. With his swimming goggles on, he took a long look at the fantastic shape of her body shimmering between water and light. He surfaced again for air. For her. She was swimming away, though, swimming past him and their possible destiny.

That was when he heard the people on the nearby boat call her name.

"Mara, is that you?"

"Yes!" she said.

"Come aboard!" they invited.

He dove back deep in the water and smiled at the beauty of it all even as he shifted his body and swam on his back while watching the sun pierce the top layer of the sea. Eyes open behind the goggles he witnessed the steady stream of bubbles that projected from his mouth and nose, each bubble loaded with the full expression of his joy.

That boat was his.

Those friends of hers were his friends. She was to be his, he thought. It was meant to be.

Her skin felt warm under the sun as she sat among her friends on the emerald green pillows. She stared at his long, slender, and muscular body emerging from the waves and making its way up to the deck. She saw him walk toward her, shaking his wet hair, goggles around his neck, as the teak captured the imprint of each wet step. He wrapped himself in a towel, the same color as hers.

"Hello, swimmer!" he said jokingly.

"Hello, diver!"

Now they had met. The trajectory had been corrected. They could not unmeet.

She drank a few sips of cold beer with all of them, and a friend took her back to shore on the dinghy. "Come by later today. We're at the small house—the one in the hill by the beach, you know? Above the herd of goats. We'll all be there later today," he told her as he helped her off the boat.

She had lunch with her parents at the family's house under trees recently pruned that let the sun, and at night the stars, find windows among the branches. The wind blew softly, a whispering sea breeze.

She and her mom cooked with the help of the gardener's wife. That modicum of help made all the difference. The women could stay seated at the table during the meal and the chores of cleaning up disappeared as the smiling lady helped all.

After lunch, Mara went to the beach near the goat herd and swam one more time in the translucent water. The sun shone directly into the shallows as she walked out. She took a picture with her phone, each dot of white light on the crest of the low waves like a facsimile of human semen on the glimmering surface. She would send that image back to him in New York. He knew, better than anyone, what these signs meant.

Earth

WALKING AWAY FROM THE SHIFTING pebbles and sand, she found solid ground on her way up the hill. She could see the small house ahead. Her girlfriend followed her. She's the one who snapped the perfectly timed picture of the wind picking up Mara's silk pareo as it floated up, allegedly in a gust of wind. With gusto! she thought as she looked at the image. Having no replacement for her wet bikini she was naked under the pareo. Maybe, just maybe, she had unconsciously forgotten it. "For being naked is the fundamental attitude of the Greek islands," she had told him once. She decided to also send that picture to him. When she got to the house, the place was bursting with energy—all the friends from the boat were there and many others as well.

The balancing act between the two of them is quite remarkable. She feeds him plots, stages, and characters, but rarely substance. He then transmutes all her musings into a story, like drawings into a painting—all the while seducing her over and over, day after day, in order to keep her love. For love, even deep love, can be fickle. She could possibly fall for the presence of the flesh, the kisses that are here rather than the promises from a world away.

She did not understand at first. She still does not, really. She is slowly realizing that this balancing act has become an important part of their routine when she is traveling alone. If she does not exude a flow of stories that fulfill his imagination, he may find them elsewhere. And she's very jealous of that. So she feeds him, hard. And he sublimates this even harder. They work at it. Slowly climbing a fantastic ladder of purely instinctual behavior.

Like an Old Soul, he gathers strength from her emotions. Even from afar, he can feel her breath speeding up as she watches the owner of the boat appear shirtless.

The boy she swam with this morning walked in from the kitchen, carrying a tray of glasses filled with white wine for everyone. This is his house, she finds out from someone else. This and all the land below, down to the pebbles and the beach. He is wearing black pants, a fabric so thin that you can see he is naked under it. She can perceive his fullness with one glance, as if she ran her fingers along it.

She has been coming to this island every August for years now. She has a personal connection with the land. She knows the hidden pathways that lead to the small shepherd sheds, those huts surrounded by olive trees where she can buy the day's goat cheese, pay with a smile and a wave of her raised hand, and then swing her hips back down the path. She also knows the maze-like streets of the town of Hora, perched high on the slopes of the mountain, just below the imposing monastery. The narrow alleys seem to wind up upon themselves. She has dinner plans in Hora with her parents tonight.

In the distance of his own water, it is his turn to swim. Time zones oblige. Here the water is cooler, and there are a few jellyfish as well, but it has to happen. He has to go for that swim.

He too will go through the elements. And in that swim, he will weave through what she has sent him so far—water, earth. He will fill the voids stroke after stroke.

The cool water feels good as soon as he starts moving in it. He gets his arms rotating at a steady pace and then lets his mind wander to the earth upon which she is standing. He can imagine her leave the back of the house and lean against the inviting fig tree, the ground around it surrounded by ripe fallen fruits. She picks a fig from a low-lying branch, peels it away and feels the flesh deposit all of its seeds on her tongue.

The young man in the thin black pants served everyone another round of wine. His grandfather had started the winery, he explained to the girl seated in front of him. She smiled at him, her eyes on the short glass he was holding, filled to the brim and level with his belt. The glass. The belt. Her eyes moved across the flat naked surface of his body, following it as it disappeared into the black fabric. She could see the curve of his hips. She saw the two veins coursing downwards just below his skin and into his nakedness below the trousers. She smiled wider. He smiled back, turned around, and walked back to the kitchen.

From the small window, he saw Mara eating the fig. He opened the door and went to her. Walking nonchalantly, arms swinging along his sides, he reached her. With crimson lips and no words spoken, he shared the fruit with her.

In the Atlantic water, her man was swimming. Watching his arms penetrate the surface over and over.

Catching up—his stroke and her story.

Under the fig tree, filled with the aroma of the utmost decadent sweetness, she did with her hands what her mind had only imagined moments ago. She thought of it, thought of it intently and it happened. It was seamless. It was simple. It was meant to be.

Eve must have fed Adam a fig. That would have been much more allegorical than a plain apple. Look at the fig: it is soft and contained, both feminine and masculine. Legend has it that, after they took a taste of the forbidden fruit, Adam and Eve saw their respective nakedness and were ashamed. Hence, the fig leaf. Yet another reason why the original fruit must have been a fig!

Kabbalah teaches us that the nakedness they experienced in the Garden of Eden was not that of simple exposure of skin, but rather that they were able to see into each other's soul and essence. That they were transparent to each other, naked to each other in other words. They could read each other's thoughts, feel each other's emotions. Once the harmony was shattered, it was too much to bear, and they became opaque to each other. The last vestige of their previous transparence residing thereafter in the translucence of their nails.

Every Friday evening, upon lighting the Shabbat candles, men and women observe the reflection of the little flame on their nailbeds. A reminder of the garden of Eden.

Mara was in such a garden just then. Her lips over his. Her hands running up and down his bare chest and broad swimmer's back. She loved feeling how strong his body was. The smell of his skin, an earthly mixture of plants and wet earth, was intoxicating. His tanned skin still tasted of salt as she let her tongue touch him, her face deep in his neck.

It was fast. It was slow.

She had him rest against the trunk of the tree. The cactus flowers had bloomed that day, only to die later the same night; she knew what her husband would want her to do.

With her glass empty, the girl he had spoken to moments ago on the veranda walked into the kitchen as well. From the square window, she witnessed Mara's mouth slip easily over his manhood, his cock jutting out from unbuttoned pants, belt still on, flesh raised through the open fabric. He held onto a branch with one hand, his head back to the sky. With the other hand, he held the back of her neck. It was over as quickly as she wanted it to be. She felt the taste and pulled back to see the glorious white arc of seeds arch to the sky and splash on the earth, right by the over-ripened open figs.

On a nearby tree a pearl-gray dove seemed to be watching as well.

It was oniric, a fabulous fantasy in the flesh.

Now the flame had to shine brighter. He had to come back from his morning swim to write and make it happen again. For him, for her, for both of them and all the others.

He picked up his towel from a huge, beached tree trunk. Further out, a swollen sailboat was streaming away. Other-

wise, he was alone.

These cold waves here, so far from hers.

In his mind, he had to make them merge.

Fire

SOME MEN ARE MADE OF FIRE. **Deep in, they burn. It is a desire to desire.**

They made gods out of this, gods who molded metal in the hottest of furnaces. A god for each action, each emotion at first, until only one could be present. And that One, only in his absence. He retracted himself, herself, from the world. The Zimzum, they call it. Leaving only a single ray of passionate light in the world.

From Mount Olympus, Zeus, the king of gods, would send lightning in the world. Lightning struck the city of Hora that night.

As planned, she had dinner with her parents and their friends. It was a lovely affair full of laughter and ouzo and the white flesh of freshly caught fish. A throng of people were walking by the crowded *platia*, the central square in Hora. It made for fun people-watching from their table. Mara was not facing the crowd. She did not see him walk by, almost within her breath.

She may not have seen him, but he saw her. He recognized her hair flowing along her shoulders, hair that grew like a cascade of flames. It is long and streaked, blonde by the kiss of sun.

The meal was over, Mom and Dad left, and she stayed behind with her friend. She had told her about the stories, about the need to feed the beast within her husband. Her friend had laughed. It seemed crazy, so disruptive. How can anyone survive such a relationship?

"So, repeat this again for me. You have to seduce or get seduced, and then let yourself slide along the slopes of a new passion—for his sake?" the friend asked.

"Yes."

"I'm worried. That is insane!" the friend laughed.

Not really insane, Mara thought. It works. It works for all. It spreads love in the world. It makes the rays of light brighter.

There were risks. The men could fall in love. But usually, they did not in these stormy circumstances; and if they did, *tant pis!* Or *she* could fall in love. And she always did a little. Women do that.

With each time she did though, she resurfaced, loving her husband even more. Feeling stronger, more secure, and more beautiful. And the more beautiful and secure she was, the more he loved her.

How could she explain that to a friend who did not even have a boyfriend at that moment? "He is behind you," her friend told her.

"Who?"

"The guy. The owner of the house we went to today. He's looking at us."

Mara had not mentioned the afternoon's events to her friend. No time, no real desire. She remained very private, even in her debauchery.

There he was, in white pants now. No underwear once again. She immediately noticed. He sat down at their table. She smiled coyly as she got up and excused herself, telling her friend that she would be right back.

Back home, the ospreys are teaching the young ones to hunt. They can fly. Now they need to fend for themselves.

When she came back, the two of them were talking as she expected. She placed something in her friend's purse since she was not carrying one and started to exchange pleasant words with the swimmer. Her friend checked the purse. In it Mara had deposited, almost as a reliquary, the black thong she was wearing under her dress. The friend looked at her purse in disbelief and laughed. "What are you laughing about?" he asked.

"It is for me to know and you to discover!" she answered, looking at Mara.

They walked away as a group. There was a party, he said, a few houses away. Soon they were on a glowing white terrace illuminated by the moon and a million stars. People were dancing to a Kazy Lambist song. No one seemed to have a care in the world.

He was very attentive to her, making sure her champagne glass was filled at all times and that the wind was not too cold on her exposed skin. She was wearing a low-cut black dress that elegantly revealed the seductive slope of her breast. The see-through fabric had a mixed floral pattern. The black flowers covering all the necessary parts, except if you were in the right light.

The girl who had watched them earlier from the kitchen was in the crowd as well. She came closer. She spoke to Mara's friend, wanting to know more about Mara. The friend said little, but the girl stayed anyway. It allowed her to be closer to both Mara and the boy, and to their evident nakedness, even in evening clothes.

Back home he is running along asphalt streets and dirt roads, among trees and grass, the scent of earth lingering as he prepares his mind.

A hot outdoor shower warms him up at first and then his naked body gets closer to the hearth, a beautifully suspended fireplace where he now builds a fire, seven hours behind.

He blows on the nascent flames.

She stands up and walks a few steps away, in order to better see the river of moon in the sea, she says. Actually, she did it to give him the pleasure of appreciating, from his seated vantage point, her partially hidden nakedness. She knew what she was doing. She always did.

Later, she walked up the narrow streets of Hora, lifting the dress mid-thigh to climb the steps and the steep slope. He stood behind her, his friends following from afar. They were walking upward in the city to better see the stars in the pitch-dark sky. She still held a glass of champagne in one hand. The other was busy holding the fabric of her dress just high enough for him to guess but not fully see. Pretending to fix her sandals, she let the group go ahead of her and took him by the hand, leading him to a *dédale* of streets—a maze made for bulls like him, and for sacrificial victims like her.

By the rising fire, he added dry wood. Very dry logs that burst in combustion as soon as they hit the flame. The blaze was set.

The waves were slowly linking themselves to each other. His and hers.

Far away, time was coalescing as the young man took her hand and spun her around.

The ospreys were clamoring in joy, a thrill cry of happiness. The young one might have caught his first fish. The sky was filled with their voices.

In Hora, he took her against the wall, right there in a public but isolated space. She offered no resistance. His tongue on her, in her. His cock out. She could feel the vigor in it. The hardness, metallic and soft all at once. She spread her legs and faced the wall.

She let the eagle catch his prey.

The heat was spreading through the room, the fire raging by now. His bones finally warming up from the early morning Atlantic swim.

From the corner of her eyes, she saw the girl.

She did not know that this same girl had witnessed them earlier. She did notice the smile on the girl's face as she approached, closer and closer. Close enough now to kiss her with that smile. Mixing tongue to tongue. And with her hands, the girl grabbed the naked manhood, forcefully pushing it into the spread-out prize. She then took her own top down, revealing beautiful small breasts with large nipples and brought them to Mara's mouth for her to kiss and lick. The three of them casting shadows of lust and love and desire on the bleached white walls of ancient houses. A black-and-white projection of intense pleasure. His hand found the new girl's inner legs. He slipped his belt off. And in unison, they moved together. Finding their synchronized beat from the nearby music.

Up on Mount Olympus, the Greek gods were watching them. Prometheus blowing on the fire in his sacred box.

On the nearby cactus, the flowers stayed open a little longer.

She was wet. And when he asked her much later if she'd come, she lied a little and denied it. For in fact, she was coming all day. During her morning swim in water, while enveloped in the scent of earth later in the day, and finally, in the delight of fire in the night. She'd come over and over: a long orgasm of pure central pleasure. And finally, she'd come hard against the walls of the narrow street. Taken in a public place by a modern Minotaur, deep in her center, a silent moan emanating from both their lips.

Air

THE WIND COVERS EVERYTHING. And air recovers it all. Forgives all.

From high above, the ospreys watch. Here, and in Greece. It's their turn to observe.

From above, as from below, a different line of sight reveals a different story.

There is his version, and then there is hers. The birds fly into the same air that carries their love, in words and images. They fly right through the electronic waves and absorb all—love, lust, her passion, and his imagination.

The air becomes ubiquitous.

He felt her pleasure, her orgasm, even before she lied about it to him.

The air is there. It cannot lie. Each breath linking the two of them as they seesaw on the magical toy plank between reality and barely formed fiction.

Epilogue

He was enjoying one last swim. Soon he'd be picking her up from the airport. He could see jets high up in the air. He can imagine her in one of them, flying back to him now.

The planes landed, one after the other, each pregnant with passengers, all with their own stories.

He wanted to hear hers, to see her face as the words spilled out of her lovely lips. See her eyes smile as she gently lied—

sometimes to embellish, sometimes to seemingly protect him, sometimes without even knowing she did. Every passing moment was further erasing her last few memories. He wanted to capture her as soon as she was back to him. Back in his arms, back in her voice.

All she wanted was to be captured. "Please take me back close to you, back to us," her body screamed. She was close, but she was still lost in the midst of all the logistics of traveling, customs, suitcases, health checks, and New York airport grime. And then finally, she found his arms. His smell, his scent, his touch, all that she had so longed for. And his strength as he lugged the heavy suitcases into the back of the Range Rover, and then again as he squeezed her hard against his chest one more time before the ride home.

They spoke a little of everything on the ride back. He heard nothing—in his mind, he kept hearing over and over the same song he had played while stoking the fire back at the beach house a few hours before. He heard the music. She was the fire now.

She has two luxuries whenever she comes back from these trips. The first is that she can leave the suitcases at the door of their flat. In the morning, Clara, the housemaid, will open them, wash and fold the myriad lightweight choices she packed, and put everything back in its proper place. The next luxury is entering her own shower, turning on the hot water, and letting the stream cascade down the back of her neck and her body until it is warmed up and completely wet. When she can wait no longer, she finally gets her face and long hair wet as well. At that instant she moves from darkness into light.

She is home.

He was waiting for her. She was in no rush. He was always ready.

Her hair still slightly damp, combed back behind her, her skin soft with body oil, she slipped naked into their bed. Well, not completely naked. Wearing a leopard print camisole, and with the stealth of that animal, she found her way to him. She left everything behind and was almost all his once again.

They could have made sweet love and without words fall asleep in each others' breath. They were both tired. There was no shame in a gentle, homecoming reconnection sex. It just was never going to happen. He knew that bringing anything up at a later date was a bad idea.

He entered her sideways, legs crossed over each other. This way he could be in her and caress her crest at the same time. Their heads were lying close to each other on the same pillow. He could see her face, her lips, his body gradually adjusting to hers. And in turn, hers to his.

The same deep rhythm was playing. The dimmed lights were there without being really here. Like God, he smiled.

After the introduction, the appetizer, the pure physical pleasure of her presence, the feel of his manhood in her, the sensation of seeing and rediscovering the beauty of her being and her young body, hardly five minutes later, he leaned to her ear and asked the magical question. "My baby, my love, were you a good girl for me?"

"Yes," she moaned back, her hips riding up and down on him. She enjoyed the motion and could have gone on like that for much longer, but his voice was like a jolt, forcing her mind to drift back to his words. She knew him. She knew he was on a mission. And she knew what to do.

Her whole being fully in tune with his, she was back where he wanted her to be: back to the island beach house by the hill, with the open black pants, and the streets of Hora with their white-washed walls. And the girl. She told him all as he kept asking.

"Yes."

She had been a good girl. Yes, a very good girl.

She could feel his cock go where the other man had been. She liked that power of repetition. She liked to feel him hard and even harder as her words became ever more descriptive. She was in control. He was on top of her. The weight of his being on her hips, his chest high above her, where she could revel in his broad shoulders and feel the tenderness of his nipples.

And then she was no longer in control.

She had to be punished now. She had been good, which was bad. And when she was bad, that was good. Blindfolded, her arms and legs spread apart by the rope, her camisole raised above her midsection, she waited for the lashes of his belt. Her ass was still red from the other belt. That sight made him even harder. He slapped her and then kissed her, kissed her cheeks, kissed her thighs. His tongue found the savory taste and went deep into her. When he kissed her mouth a little later, she could taste herself again. She found herself again.

It had been a long, beautiful trip.

ENDURANCE

S HE WAS RADIANT JUST STANDING there, and radiant again as she walked, building with each step another arch for an insatiable temple. Her bare feet landed softly along the cobblestone path. She walked as if to caress the air that surrounded her, and when she moved, her hips swung side to side, and when she stopped, her hands came to rest gracefully on them.

She had the gait of past Nubian women who were once sold to wealthy owners and then bred over generations along the different Mediterranean coasts. As such, she walked with their same grace, confidence, and elegant ease merging together with each move she made, a confluence of cultures and time- a thousand steps a day. A thousand dreams a day.

The shooting crew was sitting at a café by the harbor. It

was a small group, but they were good at what they did. They had been flown to the island for a few days' work and were hoping to complete the whole shoot on the first day.

Today was promising, with no major clouds in the sky. It was still early in the morning and the night's coolness was lingering along the edge of the harbor. She could smell the earth with its plants and flowers as the rising sun warmed them up. She could smell the sea and its saltiness, floating on the breeze. Soon, the golden hour of crisp, early morning light would smoothly fill the space between villas and yachts. Like honey, she thought. As she looked up, the assistant cameraman was placing a full spoon of the local honey in his mouth. She smiled at the coincidence. And then she lost her smile when he took the same spoon and dipped it again in the honey jar. It was a small thing, but she felt it somewhere deep in her—an intrusion. Human saliva mixing itself within the almost living organism of the bees' gift. It reminded her of past dips, of past intrusions.

She brushed it off. She was good at that. She had to be. They wanted a model with a positive attitude, and she would deliver. The early morning air pricked at her cheeks. She was glad she'd brought her jacket. The silk felt good on her skin. The garment wrapping itself smoothly along her body. Under it, she wore almost nothing, as they had asked her to. The jacket itself was cut in an oriental style, with no collar and small wooden pegs that slipped as buttons into a loop of the pink fabric. It kept her warm and it caressed her inner thighs when she moved a little, secretly soothing her.

Somewhere above the café, someone was streaming electronic music. Seemed early for that. But then again, maybe it was just late for them. Her hips swayed gently, almost spontaneously, with the rhythm.

Everyone in the crew was quiet, sipping espressos and absentmindedly looking at the yachts: each yacht a bubble of wealth connected to the side of the pier by a thin platform of wood, a tenuous bridge between our world and theirs. All the boats were lined up together in a row, spectators and actors at once—incredible sophisticated machines of floating steel whispering to whoever was watching:

Leave your shoes before you step onboard. Leave all your prejudices on the cobblestone and walk the plank to me. Come, feed on me.

They finished their coffees almost in unison, the cups of white ceramic making a faint clinking noise as the bottoms of the cups found their way into the grooved rims of the matching plates.

She saw an ant crawling on the tabletop and, as she stood up, she blew it discreetly to safety. It was showtime, and languorously she stretched her long, slender body towards the sky. They had picked her for her positive attitude, but also for her marvelous body. Actually, and she knew that well, mainly for the body.

The assistant cameraman, the guy with the spoon of honey, watched her as she turned toward a small canvas suitcase. She felt his eyes on her. She turned around, and looking back at him said, "Are you checking me out, darling?"

And with that single sentence, he knew he would never sleep with her. It was not the "Are you checking me out" part that revealed it. It was the "Darling." So sanguine.

Before the full bikini shoot, she had to do a trial walk. She slipped on the strapless golden heels and took her jacket off. Mauve—that was the color of the lining. Mauve. The color of Monet. A color between two worlds. A vibration rather than a pigment. Like a choice between two realities. Underneath, she had a leopard-print bathing suit that seemed to melt along her curves and mold itself in between them. She removed the jacket and started her walk. The whole place went totally silent. Even the makeup artist, a woman who had seen it all, was speechless. She was stunning. She emanated a spirit of Savannah mixed in with the elegance of a luxury house of couture. Decadent and delectable all at once. She did not wait for the silence to break, and she stepped forward, moving into the rapidly expanding light and sending long tangential shadows along the white outline of the moored yachts.

The photographer moved away from her, moved to where he was supposed to be positioned, and followed her with the lens. He flipped a switch, and for his own pleasure, he started filming her. Not photographing her as he should have been, but filming her while she walked, and moved. Others were doing it as well. Phone cameras were being pointed at her, one after the other, from spectators lined up on the side of the cafés, and from the crewmen of the yachts on the other side of the pier. The electronic music grew louder. They had seen her from their window, and now the loudspeaker was facing the boats. Everyone was staying at a distance. This was a European city, and they understood the concept of space and privacy.

Oblivious to the growing crowd, she did her practice run, looked at the fashion photographer, and motioned she was ready. Her head was tilted slightly to the side, as if to avoid the rising sun on her face. She lowered her dark, thick-framed sunglasses and, in doing so, released her hair, feeling as if the very motion of her long hair cascading down her naked shoulders was being slowed down by the silence in her head. Meanwhile, her slightest of movements were being captured by the countless digital screens aimed at her and her near-nakedness. She thought of her love, her lover, and everything was exactly where it was supposed to be. Whatever followed would just fall in place.

The photo shoot was almost done—six different bathing suits, each more revealing than concealing—the golden hour waning away, and she was ready to stop. The faintest of sweat beads were appearing along the line of her hair, now pulled back in a ponytail. Having lost their decorum, people were trying to get closer to her. It was becoming increasingly difficult to change behind the handheld curtains. And the sailors and crewmen were starting to whistle. She put the silk jacket back on and made her way to the table. New espressos were brought out. She leaned back on the classic caned chair. She could feel the pattern of the caning through the thin fabric. It felt good in the cool shade under the dark blue awning.

She ordered an iced cappuccino, assuming it was going to be her only decadence for the day.

It was the assistant cameraman, the "Darling" guy, who gave her the little parcel. It was wrapped just perfectly: a small, chocolate brown paper box with a dark blue ribbon. When she asked, he said, "One of the crewmen from a yacht handed it to me for you. He left without another word," he added.

She looked at the box and smiled as she realized it somehow almost matched the color of her cappuccino, especially when she raised the translucent cup to her lips and saw the blue awning at the same time. She was no stranger to random gifts, but there was a definite air of mystery about this one.

All eyes were on her, and so, not even paying real attention to it, she casually put the parcel in her handbag. It was light yet had weight. Something seemed to move in it. Somehow, it made her think of the ant earlier in the morning. Things always seemed to somehow link themselves around her, forming a web shaped by the connection of all the dots of her existence through a thin silvery thread—her halo.

She had lived true love. And she had experienced real passionate lovemaking. Sex that had brought her to the apex of all her senses, eclipsing all others. What happens to people who never live this? How can they relate? Their life remains forever limited by their utmost experience, and that experience may be a pale reflection of the real thing. But beware those who do experience it. They face a new quandary. They have to seek it over and over again. And they may also realize that, as great as it is, it may be even better somewhere else, with someone else.

Is it better to be doomed by lack of knowledge? Ignorance is bliss, they say. Or to live it at least once, to live it to the fullest once in your life. To give back to nature all the powers that were invested in you when you reached this earth. To enjoy life and your physical self to such an extent that all else becomes *extinct*. No more fears. No more questions. The answers blowing in the words of songs on the wings of the wind: to remain alive in a flow of desire, of adventure.

None of this was really resonating within her as she stood up, but it was all there. It lived around her, around her aura. In her case, you could feel her charisma from a distance, and once again they all stopped talking as she walked back inside the café.

Her bag, containing the mysterious package, hung low over her shoulder. It had once been her mother's bag—suede with fringes. Very hippie. Very chic again nowadays. Another thread in her silver web.

She entered the café, and her eyes adjusted to the darkness of the back room, her pupils dilating instantly. Not "fixed and dilated," as she had heard her neurosurgeon boyfriend describe some patients. No, dilated with *life,* and now looking at the contents of the box with marvel. It was not the cut-off diamond bracelet she was marveling at. It was the note that had come along with it that really astonished her. Hand-written on thick white paper, it read, *Please join me tonight for a full night of adventure, and the remainder of this bracelet is yours to keep.*

It was not signed, but there was a name at the bottom of the note. She remembered seeing it on one of the boats in the harbor: *Endurance.*

She recognized that name. Her boyfriend had been reading the story of an explorer, and his boat was also called *Endurance.* Looking at the fragment of bracelet, she could see where the scissors had cut the thin silver chain, leaving only two sizable diamonds on each side of the cusp.

She walked back to the table, trying to look composed and at ease. She was anything but at ease. In her confusion she had forgotten that she still had the fragment of the bracelet in her right hand, resting between her fingers, almost like a ring.

The crowd at the table was busy looking at a kid juggling all kinds of objects with extraordinary skill and speed. He performed for a few coins. The entire crew was mesmerized—everyone but the makeup artist. She was looking intently at the snapped jewels as the model sat next to her. "Those are extraordinary stones," she told her. "So pure. So white! My father was a diamond dealer. I practically grew up among them. I can tell you these are amazing! The size alone is remarkable, but they seem flawless as well. I love the pear shape," she added as she gave the jewels back. "Where did you get them?"

"It was a surprise from my boyfriend," she responded hastily as she slipped the stones into the inside pocket of her shoulder bag.

"Well, he's a keeper!" smiled the older woman with a nod of appreciation, adding, before she too watched the juggler, "A complete bracelet like this is worth a small fortune."

She left the table quietly, and no one noticed her pink silhouette as it rounded the first corner.

Soon after she reached her small but charming hotel room. The hotel owner had moved her to it once he caught a glimpse of her. It was on the third floor and had a small balcony overlooking the courtyard of a church. Further to the right was the church tower, with its ubiquitous non-working clock dial. From her terrace, you could see the tops of the boats, but you could not see their names. What difference does it make? she thought. I'm not doing it at any rate. Silly to even think about it, she told herself. Her heart was still pounding harder than the noise her footsteps had made as she ran back. Looking around the room, she realized she had forgotten her canvas bag. It's OK, she thought. The makeup woman, Vivian, would bring it back to her. She texted her.

I'm such a mess! she thought. A real mess. But she smiled. She almost texted her boyfriend. She just could not do it. "What should I tell him?" she asked out loud while looking at the leather pouch where she kept the diamonds. She could not hold them, not yet. She took a shower instead, almost cold. Keeping her hair dry at first. And then, as the water got warmer, she let it all go. She relished the hot stream, slowly moving her body in it—feeling a twinge of excitement that gradually appeared within her despite her misgivings, despite everything else. "It would be, it *could* be, like this shower!" the words echoed around her as she thought them out loud.

Submerge yourself in the water, just put your whole head in it, let yourself be surrounded by the flow and give in. And then the water will leave you, and by then you will be yourself again.

She wrapped her hair in a towel and her body in a thin cotton robe. Almost in a dream state, she put cream on her still-moist skin, and she sat at the edge of the bed. She looked outside, deep in thought. And then she laughed—there, out there on the balcony of the church tower, right under the dial, was the hotel owner. He had binoculars in his hands. He was searching. Of *course*, he gave me this room! she thought. Men are so pitiful sometimes! she concluded, not for the first time. But somehow, she did appreciate his effort. He appeared too fat to be dangerous. He looked like a lost medieval monk out there, looking for a glimpse of truth, a shred of beauty. She paid no further attention to him. Her mind was far too preoccupied. What if the owner of that boat was obese? How could she possibly deal with that? She realized she was worrying about it, as if she was actually considering doing it. She could not believe that she kept thinking about the whole thing. Yet she did. Inexorably, the unexpected proposal came charging back at her.

In the lobby, she told the man at the desk, who was also the bartender and the night watchman, to have the maid make up her room and, while up there, wave at the man standing on the church's tower.

She had hardly taken two steps outside the small hotel when she bumped into Vivian, coming towards her with her canvas bag. They handed it to the man at the desk, who, aside from being everything else was also the hotel porter. Back outside, they made a right turn and walked together uphill towards a tight cluster of pine trees visible above all the houses. Vivian had said she had wanted to explore it. The walk up was not easy. How do the locals manage it? she wondered. Not only was it steep, so steep that at places they had to climb steps, but years of footsteps and weather had smoothed the stones to a slippery finish.

Finally, they reached the trees. Those were her favorite pine trees. They had sweeping, sweet-smelling low branches, and instinctively she let her hand caress the soft needles. Higher up on the rocks she could see other pine trees standing like parasols against the blue sky. "Like a shaved pussy," her boyfriend had once said of them. Thinking about that made her finally smile again.

They sat down together on a stone bench, and only then did she realize that the place was also a graveyard—very small, very private, and obviously belonging to a family that had refused to be buried close to the church or been forbidden to. For that moment, she did not want to know. She wanted things to stop spinning in her head. She looked straight ahead. Looked at the waves beginning to form in the distant water. They were innocent ripples at that distance, but she knew they would eventually rise and, in a crescendo of power, submerge everything as they crashed along the shore. She kept looking ahead. Vivian was silent, as if she intuitively knew she had to be.

She looked hard for a few moments longer and then, her face softened. She told Vivian everything. She had wanted not to. Telling one person is telling the world. But she did. They all do eventually. All humans want to share. That is what makes them human. The willingness to become vulnerable even when you do not want to. Animals do not share; they must defend themselves in order to survive.

Vivian listened, almost did not seem surprised. She read it all so well—jeweler's daughter and mature woman all in one. There even seemed to be the hint of a smile at the corner of her mouth. She said nothing for a long while. They sat looking afar at the sea and, closer, at the small gravestones, and listening to the pines humming overhead in the wind.

Vivian broke the silence. She said, "You know, even though my sister is the one who took over our dad's business, I still know my stones pretty well, and these are exquisite. They would be rather valuable and easy to sell on the market."

She spoke clinically, without any extra layer. Not what you'd expect from a makeup artist, she thought to herself, and she continued to listen as Vivian went on.

"Based on the fragment you showed me there may be another five stones, maybe six or seven. They would all add up to a magical number," she reflected out loud. "Lucky eight for the Asian market, but seven or nine for the Western world."

She heard herself say, "Yeah, but what if he's fat and gross?"

To which Vivian answered, "The owner may be overweight but unlikely gross, for this was very elegantly put together. From the box wrapping to the subtle hint of money."

"Yes, but the proposition itself is gross."

"Only if you assume that experiencing a highly unusual

moment is unnatural. The proposition is risky but understandable. The yacht owner may never get a chance to see you again. And once you were seen, you were desired. Highly desired. It takes a highly motivated person to pursue it with such vigor. This was not a cheap proposal. I reckon the stones themselves will be nearing the three-quarter-million mark."

There was silence again.

"But maybe what they want me to do will be gross."

"It's one night only, and you tell them that someone in the harbor knows that you are onboard. And that they will report if anything seems out of line, or if you do not show up at a certain time and give the thumbs-up sign, or something like that."

She left Vivian on the bench and went over to the two gravestones. Weeds had taken over most of their unkempt surfaces. It must have been a couple, she thought. She could not figure out the names in the aged inscriptions but lost her breath when the only words that came through were *"marriage de diamant"*.

The couple must have been married for at least sixty years, hence the reference to diamonds.

She returned quickly to the safety of Vivian's presence, hesitated, and then told her about the unbelievable coincidence of words.

Vivian said nothing, letting it all settle somewhere. And then she took the girl's hand and said, "I will keep an eye out if you want. I can see the boats from my hotel room, and with binoculars I could watch guard. Maybe the hotel has binoculars."

"Oh, yes they have," she sighed, remembering the proprietor. "They do for sure."

They sat down again in the shade. It almost felt good then, as if the whole thing had been settled, and they never really spoke about the ethics of it. It was settled and that was it.

She wanted it to be over.

"Will you help me?" she asked Vivian.

"Sure thing."

"I mean getting dressed and all that."

Vivian smiled and took her hand, and that was that.

Maybe tonight would be horrific, maybe tremendous. Either way, she could make in a few hours the equivalent of two years of hard-working salary. Hard work with people always trying to touch her, to caress her, to bump into her. Two years versus a few hours.

"Maybe it would even be fun," she thought, not realizing she had said it aloud.

"It will be fun if you make it fun. The best way to predict what will happen is to make it happen." She added, "Take the lead if you can."

And on those words, they slipped back safely to their hotel.

The preparations seemed royal. Vivian did everything for her. She washed her hair, combed it, and dried her body with soft linens that she said she always traveled with.

She let Vivian take care of everything, her hands running

along her long, perfect body, almost as if preparing her for the event—like a specialty servant in Roman times before the lady of the house gets ushered into the master bedroom.

She wore a simple black thong, so small that she was almost naked even while wearing it. She then slipped on a white linen dress, not too revealing, but she knew that with the right lighting, it would become see-through, and nothing could remain hidden. Vivian finished the makeup by applying a touch of mauve on her eyelids. It made her soft eyes seem to melt even further away and gave her a very vulnerable look, as if to entice mercy of some kind.

Whatever, she thought. She would be OK, she repeated to herself. There were enough signs—the boat had the name of the book, the graves spoke of diamonds, and Vivian was there and would overlook it all from afar. Nevertheless, she did take a long sip of the cold, clear tequila from the glass Vivian brought her.

The sun had sunk, though for only a few hours at that time of year. It was time to go.

Vivian had scoped out the harbor. She told her where to find the *Endurance*. It was in the section allocated for the larger boats, and she quickly found it. It was probably the most elegant of all the yachts. Not bulky, no empty pads for a helicopter, no expensive extra toys on deck. The name written in deep blue capital letters, in the same font as a Christopher Wool painting. She liked that.

She turned back and looked for Vivian. As planned, she was stationed at her bedroom window, binoculars in hand, waving, a wave that said, "Hey, I'm here, and you're there, and now you're actually gonna do it!" She was going to wave back but she held back.

The sea was calm in the peaceful harbor, the boats protected from the waves by a long jetty that looped on itself and closed up the cove along the island coast.

She thought of the nascent, distant waves she had seen earlier in the day, high up, from the stone bench. That same body of water having traveled all the way under the boat by now. Her own body shivered ever so slightly, a muted thrill that spread right through her limbs. She took the deep breath of underwater divers and, shoes in hand, strolled up the narrow plank onto the ship.

There was no one there to greet her, so she turned toward the cabin adjoining the rear deck, her steps greeted by a thick, white woolen carpet. The walls of that cabin, which had appeared metallic when she looked at them from the outside, were actually made of thick tinted glass. Through them, she could see the harbor and the other boats. She glanced around the room. The furniture was sparse and elegant, almost invisible. "As it should be," she remarked. There was a deep white couch with soft pillows, and next to it two Jeanneret chairs made of teak and cane. A low ceramic table caught her eye. By Jouve, she thought. She wanted to run her fingers over the glaze, but just then, a tall, beautiful woman walked in—not beautiful in a purely plastic way, but beguiling, with great presence and wide lips that spread into a smile as she gently bowed to her in a welcoming greeting. She thought that this woman reminded her of someone, but she was too nervous to think about it. The woman picked up a remote that was resting on a polished wooden ledge, and music came flowing in. She could not believe it. It was the same DJ dance music that she had listened to earlier today. She was stunned for a moment, and in that moment her fear melted. *Surely this is all going to be fine.* The smiling woman would lead her, and she would meet the owner and then *just let it be.* Standing still, legs slightly apart, it was her turn to smile.

The tall woman kept looking at the silhouette framed by the rear door. The web of the dress transilluminated by the peering early evening light. It was a beautiful sight.

A FEW DAYS LATER SHE FLEW BACK and went straight home from the airport, her skin still drenched in sun and salt. She was waiting for her boyfriend to come back from a late surgical case. As time passed, she became more and more nervous. Her initial resolution to tell him all was waning. It was pretty heavy. Even though it had happened days before, the events still resonated in her, and the dance-music beat kept reminding her of it over and over again. And, she just could not stop listening to it.

What am I doing? she thought. What am I going to say?

He walked in, and the biggest smile lit up his face as soon as he saw her. She was tanned, wearing a thin, long-sleeved white shirt, and he immediately saw that she had no bra. His eyes moved down her hips and took in the rest of her, lingering on his favorite thin blue gauze skirt with the flirty edges. In no time, his lips and hands were all over her. She drank it all in, his touch purifying her. She adored him in that moment.

He wanted more, she could feel it, but she put a stop to it. She leaned back, holding onto his arms and looked into his face.

"I have something to tell you first," she said.

"Tell me later," he urged.

"No, it has to be now," she answered.

He slowed down. He settled. Her music was still playing in the background.

He changed out of his day clothes and put on his jogging shorts. He was unsure as to what she was about to tell him, and a run would be a good excuse to leave the apartment if he needed to. They went to the bedroom, and he lay down on the bed. He was calm but attentive. A look of concern shadowed his face as she settled down on the wooden Nakashima chair by the bedside instead of lying close to him.

The swallows were flying in circles outside in the dusk, high in the sky. It would be good weather tomorrow, he managed to think. He almost reluctantly turned to her and said, "Go! Tell me, baby."

"It may be a painful story," she said, but immediately added, "but it could be a good one if you enjoy it."

"Tell me, baby, best to let it out."

"Well, it all started the day of the photo shoot," she said, and then went on to explain the succession of events. How she felt, how she felt about the name of the boat and the graves, and also the sheer magnitude of the money, and how he had hinted in the past that something like that could possibly turn him on. She went on and on, her voice soft and unsteady at times, as if she was realizing the enormity of what she had done as she spoke of it out loud. She told him about the white carpet and the furniture. She knew he liked these details. She talked about the woman, too.

"Well?" he asked, "Did you leave or stay on board?"

She looked at him silently for a long time. Looked at his face as if some dramatic shift would occur after he found out. She looked at the kind beauty of his eyes, the slope of his runner's body, the hungry expression that permeated his entire being. This was going to be one of those pivotal moments that define an entire relationship, possibly define their life to come.

She stood up by the bedside, facing him, legs slightly parted, and with her right hand she unfastened the sleeve button on her left arm folded the white fabric up her wrist and forearm. There it was, catching the light, catching his gaze.

He was sitting on the bed by then, looking at her wrist only, not at her face, not at her eyes. Just at her wrist and the diamond bracelet. At that moment, the next song came from the playlist. She heard the words: *It's a beautiful day.* She was not sure if he had heard them. He had not moved yet. She could feel him think. The air itself was thick and sacred.

And then he laughed and roared at the same time and pulled her onto the bed in one big sweep. They lay side by side, and he whispered to her, "Tell me all, you filthy high-class whore."

Her heart was still racing. And she heard herself talk, the sentences flowing from her like words in a song.

"I could not believe it," she said. "The woman came to me and started caressing me, my shoulders, my hair, my hips, the side of my face. All so delicately, yet so intently at the same time. I was confused. I hadn't expected it, and I wasn't sure what I was supposed to say. I told her that, before we did anything, she should be aware that a friend was outside monitoring my activities, waiting for me to signal her. And that she would call for help, if I needed it.

"She took me by the hand and brought me to a silver-framed, black-and-white photograph of two women.

"'Oh, yes!' she said, 'you must be referring to my sister Vivian.' And when I looked closer at the photo, there she was, Vivian, staring back at me from within the frame. It was the same Vivian who had just waved at me.

"'Oh, my goodness!' I said. 'And where is the owner of the yacht?'

"'Well, that would be me,' she told me as she placed her hand under my hair and along my neck and pulled me to her. She brought her face close to me and whispered, 'And the diamonds are real,' before kissing me. We drank champagne and more tequila sitting on a hidden deck in the middle of the boat. It was almost like an implosion of sorts, a totally private space and yet open to the darkening sky. There were candles all around and, at times, a really good-looking waiter came to serve us the drinks. The music came from loudspeakers embedded throughout the boat. Her foot caressed mine as we sat at the table and ate berries and ice cream. I started to like her. She had a black silk shirt, and I could feel the weight of her breast by the pull on the fabric. She wore white linen shorts and had long, powerful legs. As she ate, she kept looking only at me. The waiter came back to check on us again, and she gave him a nod pointing to my direction. He walked to me and started caressing my face, my hair. He nudged my chair towards him, and I watched the woman lean back on her own chair, still looking at me. When I faced the waiter again, he had unbuttoned his pants."

By then, her boyfriend was holding her in his arms, caressing her thighs with one hand, stretching the fabric of her skirt over her shaved pleasure. "Keep on going," he said. "Tell me more."

"Well," she sighed, "the woman flicked her head towards

the guy's manhood, so as naturally as I could, I took him in my mouth. He got big in no time. I was trying to do a good job to impress her. I did to him what you always said I should do. I let my lips slowly slide up and down on him, luckily, he was not as big as you, so I took him whole in the back of my mouth. I grabbed his ass and pushed him even deeper, though I could barely breathe. Somehow the gag I felt was comforting, it meant something, and I only let go when I knew he was about ready to cum.

"I must have done a good job because right after, he came all over my face, thick and hot and sticky. I looked back at the woman. Smiling at me, she slowly leaned forward, and with a dessert spoon, she cleaned my face. Then she dipped the spoon in the melted vanilla ice cream, and we both ate from that same spoon."

By now her boyfriend had his fingers deep in her pussy and she pushed herself hard against the firm digits. "Go on," he said in a husky voice.

"She took me downstairs to another room. It was long and rectangular, beneath the waterline. There were lights along the outside hull, and you could see the underwater world through the thick glass walls.

"I said, 'I need to go on deck and wave to Vivian.' The woman smiled, pulled out an iPad, and there was Vivian at her post by the window.

"'Wave to her now,' she said. And as I did, Vivian waved

back and gave me a thumbs-up sign. And after that, I was told in a few words that my task was to mimic whatever she did. She called it 'drafting.' Like a cyclist or a Formula One driver. And so I drafted."

"SHE STARTED DANCING AND MOVING along the dance pole. There seemed to be a stream of men and women, too. They made love in front of us, and we danced between them. We touched them and let them touch us. I kept an eye on her and followed her lead. She was insatiable. She was testing me. Soon, my dress was off."

They too were making love by now, side by side at first, and then she moved herself on top of him so he could hear her whispers. She whispered all the filth that she had done—the cocks licked, and pussies, and an ass or maybe two. She told him a lot. She did not tell him everything, though, because she herself could not believe what she had done that night.

It had seemed all so natural at the time. It had been the right thing to do, she had felt. And all she was doing was following the lead of that woman. They kissed tequila into each other's mouth, and she accepted it all. Her body became an underwater creature surrounded by water teeming with life, and couples mating with each other like intertwined coral.

Finally, they both came back up on deck. It was pitch dark by then. Mercury and Venus hung low in the distant sky.

She did not tell her boyfriend how they had both slept on

the large outdoor bed, limbs locked in the deepest of sleep. She did not have to tell him. He had dozed away after he exploded over her words. She knew he would wake up again soon and he would want to hear it all over again. And hopefully he would accept her once more.

A little later, she rose and picked up the hidden watch from the drawer. It was a Paul Newman Daytona Rolex. He had always wanted one. This one had the white dial.

She gave him a few more minutes and then nudged him. He was always quick to wake up; the years of working emergencies had trained him to be. It took a second, but soon everything flooded him anew. He thought about it all over again, it felt somehow different now that he was spent and lucid.

She gazed at him intently. From the way he looked at her, she knew that he had forgiven her already. That is why she loved him so much. She knew he adored her.

But just in case there was a residue of doubt, she slipped the metal bracelet over his left wrist. "What on earth is this?" he asked.

"You know better than I do."

"But—but how did you get it?"

"Well, that bracelet the woman gave me, that bracelet was too big for me. So I exchanged two stones for a watch. And now it's my gift to you." She smiled.

He was looking at the dial, feeling the lightness of the vintage steel on his wrist. He looked and looked, not daring to look up yet. Thinking. Reflecting.

He heard her say, "What time is it, darling?"

He smiled. His breath made a funny laughing noise as he exhaled audibly.

He looked up at her, and smiled even wider as he answered, "It's past midnight, baby. Time to meet again."

THE HOUSE IN HORA

THE WHITEWASHED HOUSES WERE ABLAZE in the island's evening sun, interlocked and tightly connected within each other like fingers of two loving hands. He, the visiting museum curator, looked at them from way above, standing on top of the monastery's dark wall. From there the houses all seemed different, yet all looked alike.

He was lonely.

He was there alone.

Beneath him, the small city wrapped itself lovingly, like a bracelet, around the base of the monumental building. It was a jewel of a town, with the most exquisite multi-level houses facing the two bays—the moonrise bay and the sunset bay.

In one of those houses, she was getting ready for her husband.

The island itself floats in the Mediterranean, shaped like a giant three-tiered cake. At the top stands the austere monastery; the next layer is comprised of the white houses of the city of Hora, suspended on the flanks of the steep hills, laced together by narrow pathways, and centered on one small square they call the Platia. The foundation of the cake is the remainder of the island. A road snakes its way down to the harbor, the Scala. From there you can go east to find pebble beaches nestled along a carved-out coast and swim in water as clear as a clean soul.

Her husband, Adam, was riding his mountain bike back up towards Hora. It had been his idea to bring the bike along on this vacation trip. No one else seemed to own one here. He had gone down the mountain to swim in the sea, and his body was still wet and salty as he biked his way back up, flushing the pedals down with the freedom of someone who loves to ride up steep climbs, pulling up on the clips of the pedals as much as pushing down on them. He had his earphones in, the beat carrying him higher and higher.

It was tough, he realized, much tougher than he had anticipated. He understood now why there were no bicycles on the island! As it got even steeper, he stood up in the saddle, his arms pulling up on the handlebars. An open Mini Moke car overtook him. In it, young boys and girls were laughing. He caught the eye of one of the girls. It lasted an instant, a long instant, and then she was gone, short dark hair and all.

He rode all the way back up and was about to open the main door by the street level when he remembered that it was now the entrance to his wife's space in the house. It had been agreed, before they arrived, that she would have the ground floor, with its cozy bedroom and breakfast nook in the glorious green garden. He would use the separate entrance up on the third floor. He had to ride up some more and then descend a tight narrow staircase from the street and open a wooden door leading to a small vestibule. To the right stood a small, functional kitchen, and to the left a spacious salon, furnished with vintage local furniture, that led to a bedroom with views of the coast and the sea. Ahead of the vestibule a combination of small balconies and terraces spread out towards the coastline. This is where he was to have his breakfast.

The middle floor contained the main bedroom. It was a vast, magical place. The house had been built right along the edge of the mountain, and in that room large boulders were still visible on the wall, to the left when you walked in. They were white-washed and shaped like the profile of pregnant whales. They gave the room a feeling of belonging to another era, a time that never ceased to exist. To the right, three windows faced the never-ending sea.

THEY HAD AGREED THAT THEY COULD NOT MEET during the day. Those rules of engagement had been established long before they left their own home. They could only get together after sunset, in the bedroom on the middle floor. The night was theirs until the rooster sang five times. For two nights, he could choose what they did, and for the other two, she would. The last night was left to fate. This was the first time they ever did anything like this.

"How hardcore?" he had asked her.

"Everything goes," she had answered.

He brought the bike into the house through the wooden door. Tonight, the first one was hers.

He showered the salt and sweat away. He still had a few hours. He went to eat freshly caught fish and drink local white wine at his favorite taverna. High up above, from the monastery, the curator saw him walk away, not noticing him.

He was a guest curator there, on a mission from a museum in Athens to appraise medieval objects and artifacts in the monastery's collection. He was sleeping in a small alcove on the roof, with very little living space. He did not mind. Above him there was nothing else but sky, and in the darkness and stars he could follow Venus and Mars—or, more appropriately, since he was in Greece, Aphrodite and Aries. Love and War. Woman and Force. They chased each other almost playfully, and that night, even with one eye closed, he managed to see both planets. In that visual enclave they became linked once again—away from the morning sun gods and mythological judgements. Away from earthly inhibitions and taboos.

His job consisted of working long hours indoors, appraising ancient wooden sculptures—Virgin Marys surrounded by masterful folds, and the countless reproductions of the image of her son. A dramatic shift, he thought, from the marble and stone used to glorify the gods and goddesses of ancient Greece and the apparent solid state of those depictions.

Either way, he realized, the stone, the wood, they were all decaying. His job was to determine what could be preserved. They were the last vestige of a time long gone. Metal and glass had since replaced them, and those too were now being overturned by virtual clouds and electronic spaces. Each new material, each new human skill, creates a new system of belief, he thought. With each new language came words. New worlds. New religions.

He had to go swimming tomorrow. He needed it.

ADAM WOULD SOON COME DOWN to the second floor, the meeting space they had allocated for their nights together. She was ready for him. She always was, for she loved him, adored him, had for years. He made her feel whole and loved her so well! Her mind, her body—oh yes, her body! He touched her like no other, with fingers of light that took over, and after she would radiate that presence for hours.

A few weeks before, they had whispered to each other the decadent plan to come to the island: the rules, the rhythms, the oblivious lack of reason. They knew the island well and, with money no object, had independently arranged for all the logistics to fall in place.

Now, all she had to do was wait for him on her first planned night.

The sun had completed its arc. From where she stood, it *did* rotate around the earth. That is what all her senses told her. The earth was not moving. How could it? She was standing on it and could feel no motion. No, the sun was the one moving, drawing in the sky the path of days— the fiery ball fading away to finally let the evening's celebrations begin.

Adam had eaten alone. He had watched the early crowd move around the Platia. It was way too early to call it nighttime. Nothing of any substance happened on the island until much later —sometimes much, much later. As if you needed to pay your dues to the night, to remove yourself visibly and emotionally from the day and its awe-inspiring light. You had to dive into darkness, a darkness you could only find in the dead of night. He smiled. *The Dead of Night.* What a strange expression! Most likely it referred to the act of sleeping. That was supposed to be one-fortieth of death, according to his tradition. A foretaste of the afterworld.

He ate little. He knew better. His body was relaxed, with the satisfied soreness of self-imposed physical effort. He was looking forward to the night. He had no idea what to expect. In the coolness of the evening, he felt a sneeze grow within him. He let it swell and pass through him like a breeze.

A fortieth of an orgasm, he thought, smiling internally.

For now, they only communicated by digital messages. She had told him to show up at around 11:00 PM. In his world that meant *vingt-trois heures*. He liked the twenty-four-hour reading of the clock. Each hour was allocated its own personal weight. *Vingt-trois heures*—the penultimate narrow space of time before the perfectly vertical final line.

Would he be jealous? he reflected to himself. On paper, yes, but in reality, it was complex. Love is complex. Love between two people becomes even more complex. That is why so many people enjoy loving themselves only. It is easier, presents less conflict, less potential pain. And who knows, perhaps the same pleasure. He was not wired that way. He wanted someone to share his life with—Layla. He missed her already. It had hardly been a day and he missed her next to him—her flow, her flowers, her sweet body and her presence. He wrapped it all around him like a pashmina.

Vingt-trois heures.

He walked down to the second floor stone landing. It was an alcove overlooking the water in the distance and led to the second-floor bedroom. You could see no other houses from there.

A woman was waiting for him. She was dressed all in white, in a uniform pants and shirt, like a nurse of sorts. He looked at her face intently for a moment. He had seen her before, he thought. A beautiful girl with short dark hair cut with bangs, long eyelashes, and very little makeup. She invited him to lie face down on the prepared massage table. No words, just a gesture. He finished his drink and placed it on the side table among crystal sculptures of translucent amethyst and quartz. Then, he took his clothes off in front of her as instructed. She did not look away. He lowered his body, face down, on the cushioned table. It's the girl from the Mini Moke, he recalled finally as he laid down. The one he had seen earlier for an instant from his bike.

Her hands moved lightly along the course of his body to explore its full expanse, and after that introduction, she covered him with a thin sheet and continued to massage him. He could feel her hands through the fabric. It was almost more pleasurable than being naked, he thought. Almost. When she eventually uncovered him like a gift and let her bare hands lather his sore back and hamstrings with thin oils, he let a deep sigh of pure bliss slip out of him.

That is when he felt the second pair of hands.

He recognized them. They were Layla's.

The four hands covered the span of his body, it seemed, at all times. Shoulders, arms, legs, and ass. He could feel where they were and where they would go. He loved it, and that could have been plenty enough, but he knew there would be more to come, and his whole being was actually begging for more. Before the girl put oil along the arc of his ass, she kissed it, allowing her tongue to lick the long crest and then the deeper meadow. Earlier, from the car, she had admired his butt wrapped in stretched-out spandex as he rode up the steep road, alone and courageously, and now here she was, burying her face in it. Adam responded by shifting his hips, by rocking them in and out and letting her find all the pleasures, both of her hands grabbing his muscular cheeks. Layla kept on caressing his shoulders and, at times pushed the other girl's face deeper.

There was a certain continuity in their harmonized motion, as if rehearsed at a primordial level, as if in a dance. His hips, her tongue, his wife's hands. In the distance, in the darkness that surrounded all three of them, he heard the song.

Then it was Layla, his wife, left alone with him, communicating ever so gently with the kindest of caresses. Eventually, she too walked silently away from him. The room became completely still. He was alone. And then he recognized her gentle whistle. He was being summoned. He went to her.

He entered the bedroom. Layla had covered the whole room in a multitude of white furs. All soft and sweetly scented. Some short-haired ones, some with long hair, and some gray-toned ones here and there. Their mosaic patterns shimmered under the light of the tall candles.

The bed was in the center of the room, floating like a platform amid the sea of furs. On black satin sheets, he saw the massage girl. Head bowed, a leather-strap garment laced tightly around her body, she was naked and clad all at once.

The straps were cinched high along her thighs, barely covering her nakedness, and then bonding her breasts in layers of seen and unseen, her red nipples swelling under the small clamps that Layla was applying ever so meticulously. Her breasts now linked by a silver chain, she was on her knees, her hands tied behind her. He approached her, wrapped in a thin towel that hung from his hips. He noticed leather straps hanging from rings in the ceiling. As he stepped onto the bed, he grabbed those straps with his hands and hung onto them as Layla removed the towel. The girl immediately took him in her mouth, and he could see her full lips coursing up and down. He was standing legs apart over the outline of her elegant bent-over torso. Her skin was beautiful with olive tones shining through the oil. The leather bondage enhanced her. Her ass, tight and muscular, glowing in the dim light—a globe awaiting its fate.

The girl made him big in her mouth and he felt the urge build up within. He grabbed her hair, pulled her head back and tied her hands up onto the straps. She was sublime, her face reaching up to the sky with each slap of the whip, each time a moan trickling out from her wet red lips.

Layla was whipping her with the black multi-flanged leather whip. Soon he was in Layla, spreading her black stocking-laced legs, feeling her body rock with each blow she gave. She stopped and he watched her kiss the red welts on the girl's skin, slip her hand to her wetness, and kiss and lick her again.

She moved to the side, took his full manhood with one hand, and held the girl with the other.

She licked as he penetrated the bound girl, her tongue on them both. This was her night. She wanted it to be perfect.

The girl was glowing as he untied her arms and laid her back down carefully unto the black sheets, her skin sliding on the soft fabric. Layla held her legs apart. He could see the full beauty of her strapped inner thighs, like a glistening underwater open oyster, and he went deep in her. And deeper. For her to feel his full girth. For her to know how much he wanted her, how hard she made him with her obedience and glorious state of lust.

Layla had a finger on her crest, and he was pulling on the chain. The sight was unbelievable! The white walls, the furs, the black sheets, the leather straps, the shiny chain that teased her nipples, the red nail polish of the fingers that guided his cock deep in the girl's pussy and then deep in her ass, cheeks kept open by the same fingers. In and out of her, until the full circle completed itself. Until the Kundalini found its path, and he exploded on her face and lips.

He was still gasping for air when Layla kissed her face, both tongues simultaneously tasting his offering.

THE NEXT DAY, HE RODE THE ENTIRE COAST of the island. He raced down the initial hill in the early hours, leaning his bike into the twists and turns, music in his ears. He had no thoughts in his mind. It was just him, his bike, and an emotion of increasing velocity. He let go of it all in utter, simple happiness.

What a night, he reflected later as he paused at the other end of the island. What a fantastic visual gift his wife had provided him! Of course, it was a sexual gift, but really, it was a gift of stage. And great sex is about the stage. Even in its barest essence, it is about the space, the scents, the skin. It is about the effort. That is what made the bike move forward, effort. And that is what makes sex float away in repeated cascades of pleasure: the effort to be ready, the effort to be present, and to please.

And great sex occurs when fantasies are guessed. . . sometimes even acted upon.

He swam in the clear water. He wanted to savor every single moment. The sea, his body in the water, what it had done the night before. He savored it all. Just like when he was a young boy with a rock candy in his mouth and he kept it on his tongue for as long as possible.

He thought about the night to come. It was his turn. He had work to do. He rode back home.

LAYLA WENT TO THE BEACH after a late breakfast. She was content. She had decided to go alone rather than with a friend. She wanted to relive the previous night, and she could not conceive of talking about it to anyone. What she had with Adam was indescribable. She was willing to sacrifice for his love, yet she also realized that pleasing him was only one aspect of the foundation of her pleasure. There was a place in her brain that told her to live out their fantasies, to acquiesce to his stories and, even more, to create her own tales. As if she had picked him because he could and would make it all happen. As if she needed that, despite the perception that she should be satisfied with the common scenario. She just could not acknowledge or share that inner drive with anyone quite yet. Not yet.

It had not been her intent to whip the girl with such gusto. But she had, because she unexpectedly enjoyed it. And because she knew he would like it. At moments like that, she would do anything for him. Anything.

She had loved licking the girl with Adam watching. That was something she had never done before. Once she started, she could not stop. She had to taste her over and over. And then she had to taste both of them together. And finally, him on her. It had been incredible, far away from her comfort zone! The furs hadn't even been needed, she thought. But then she realized that all of it had been. The furs had created an exclusive space, a space of dampened sound and the promises of soft touch. The furs, the candles, they all became an organic part of the experience. As if locked into the world that she created for him, coming alive with the impulse of their desire.

She watched the ouzo get cloudy over the ice cubes. It was her favorite beachfront restaurant on the island. They treated her well there and she kept coming back. Her table was right upon the pebble stones, close to the water. She sat back and took in all the smells the pine trees, the sea, and the faint smell of sex on her fingers. She closed her eyes and saw the lashes, her hand lingering between her own legs, casually and innocently.

She opened her eyes and, between her and the sun, stood the outline of a handsome young face. He wanted to know if she had "Fire for his cigar?"

Fire for his cigar? What a fantastic opening line! She smiled. "Yes, dear boy, I have that for you." She invited him to sit at the table so she could finish her drink. Soon thereafter, Layla and the curator were swimming together. He was funny. She was relaxed. Her husband was working on that night's surprise, and she could afford a little time off. They went beneath a tree to find some shade after the swim. He really did smoke a cigar. He really did let his fingers linger along the stretched bikini fabric that covered her pussy. She could not believe his audacity. That was the most desirable thing about him—his tremendous desire for her, his palpable desire to do things to her.

Love loves a physical trampoline. She let him have a little fun, fanning the flames of his affection. Then she left.

"Yes, maybe I will see you again," she said. "Yes, maybe here."

"Maybe not."

And with that, she made her way back home on the blue

Mini Moke.

THE SECOND NIGHT, HE HAD ARRANGED for a beautiful crowd to gather at the house. There was a dress code: women had to wear something red and the men dark blue. Actually, all the men wore the same outfit he provided them with—dark blue pants and a white shirt. Same thin cotton pants—all commando style, same simple cotton shirt with thick buttons.

The women wore short skirts that floated, short skirts that molded, long dresses with slits, long dresses that allowed light to reveal all. Shirts open in front to below the norm, shirts open in the back. Brassieres alone. Silks and brocade, cottons from Egypt, lace, and taffeta. See-through fabrics that revealed thongs and straps, shaved naked identities, and some not. Tanned breasts with seductive nipples. Skin of different colors. All within a small, selected group. All individuals. All original. All willing.

No one, man or woman, who was willing to come to the party was expected to say no to anything. You had to make that choice before you walked in. The house was the true refuge.

Layla stood at a recess in the ground-floor garden and looked up at the house. From where she was, it seemed a formidable, layered cake of red light and fabric. The men in their dark outfits were a seemingly integral part of the house, and the women, all different blooms of flowers, its guests. *Le Rouge et Le Noir*, she thought. Stendhal would be intrigued.

She liked what she saw.

She was not surprised by the scale of it. Adam always had a tendency to go to excess in his fantasy world. He had made the lights in the house red—the bulbs were red, the glass around the candlesticks was red, the lampshades, too. The second-floor vestibule had a red carpet that led to the master bedroom.

He had even brought her favorite DJ, Jon Sa Trinxa, over from Ibiza. His music had a beat that made everyone sway to the same rhythm—heads bopping, shoulders swinging, and hips dancing. The crowd was constantly moving. People were going up and down the stairways. They met on the suspended balconies, the elevated terraces, and everywhere there were drinks—pink champagnes, Aperol Spritzes, and other colorful concoctions all with red floating seeds of pomegranate. The hypnotic music floated from floor to floor. Everyone was there to look and be looked at. Much earlier, as the day found its way back into the night and as they were getting ready for the party, the guests had looked at themselves in mirrors and realized that this was the island, the time, the moment to let go of it all, to release that inner desire to share, to move along with hands and lips. Not to stay home, not to watch another screen, not to fall asleep. They met there, together, under the same night.

The second-floor bedroom had a set of unspoken rules that existed only in that part of the house. In the red-carpeted vestibule stood a woman dressed in a white suit. She allowed people to enter the bedroom only if they came in as a couple. Some walked in, and shortly thereafter, walked out. Others stayed. They could only walk out as a couple as well.

There was an air of romanticism among the decadence; Layla could feel it. Seen from the outside, it did not appear decadent, but sumptuous—a voluptuous release of convention, a mix between a masked ball and a pagan festival, between the beautiful architecture of the magical white house and its present occupants. The beat went on as the guests moved along like gifts, at times exchanging the lightest of touches, a caress as they walked by, a hand that reached out to explore what decently could usually only be observed. She saw some reach for the shape of a slender breast, the curve of a shaped ass—all lovingly, as in a dance, a trance -which some were clearly experiencing-, the alcohol relieving the last of their inhibitions.

Layla went back up the stone staircase and saw Adam talking to the DJ. She left them alone and turned to the woman in the white suit, who said, "Of course you can go in alone. You are the mistress, after all."

The bed had been replaced by low red-velvet couches. All the lights had been dimmed to a crimson hue that emanated from old Venetian lanterns made of glass blown in the not so distant island of Murano, the heat and fire that molded that ancient glass ever so present in the light that now permeated the room and its naked linked bodies that found each other, once the eyes adjusted to the darkness, and discovered, scattered in the room, the pulsing hearts they had desired. The DJ played a remix of Leonard Cohen. "I am ready, my Lord," he sang through the loudspeakers. "A million candles burning," he added, and love came. Her head went back as she sat down and watched.

Adam walked in. She was waiting for him. She had her beautiful naked legs partially open. She was watching two young men who were gazing at her welcoming posture. She looked up and saw Adam watching her. Slowly, deliberately, making sure he could see, she pushed aside the thin fabric of her red thong, revealing in the seductive darkness, the object of their lust. The men unbuttoned. She saw them heavy with desire, her open legs a fountain of lust. They had to touch her now, find her with tongues and fingers. And she wanted all the hands.

Around them, bodies were melting into each other in a chaotic order based on approval and darkness. The two girls who had entered the room with the young men were interlaced close by in a soft embrace. Layla nodded toward them.

Adam understood her sacrifice—she would occupy the two men so he could satisfy the two women. And so he did, his hand finding them in a way that only the other sex can, all the while keeping an eye on her.

They were young men. She had seen boys like that before. She knew the power of direct allusion and display of sexual desire. They became mesmerized by her appetite. The way she grabbed them, taking them alternately in her mouth, cocks slipping out of their unbuttoned pants straight into her mouth. One, and then the other, one after the other. He watched as they both seemed to cum simultaneously on her face, on her naked breasts, on her smile.

She walked towards Adam, closer to the three of them now. Her face still jeweled, she kissed the girls, who, in turn, kissed and licked her with the recognition of familiar tastes. The three of them ended Adam.

She walked out, hand in hand with him, back to what suddenly appeared as a normal world.

AT THE SAME TIME, THE CURATOR TOOK the few steps from his room on the top floor of the monastery to the side rampart. He lit up a short Cuban cigar and leaned forward, elbows resting on the still-warm stones. At that hour, the city seemed painted around the neck of the hill. Like a Rembrandt white lace collar, he thought, or maybe Frans Hals. A delicate white lace blotted in one spot only, he noted, by an edifice striped in red —like an exotic flower.

He left the monastery early the next day. It was a light day at work since the other curators were absent. He went to the same beach and waited under the same tree. All day he waited. He ate alone. He drank ouzo alone. He swam alone. He was alone but he did not feel lonely, just melancholic, not because he was by himself but because she did not show up. In his mind, it was his fate to see her again. And so he stayed on and waited.

When she finally showed up, he did not reveal his elation. He looked up at the sky and let her gorgeous frame cover his horizon.

"Would you care to go on a kayak ride?" she asked.

"I was waiting for you to go," he answered with a smile.

They climbed into the small boats, and she led him around the rocks. They followed the edge of the bay. The waves were light. He looked at her as she led him, paddling ahead. He let his hand drift in the water. He was trying to contain himself.

He was going mad for her. He loved the way she moved, the way her shoulder blade slipped on her tanned back. She had removed her top, unafraid of the late afternoon sun. He could see the delicious curve of her chest in short bursts of visual angles. Like the folds of the wooden Madonna sculptures, he thought. He went wild when she landed ahead of him on the shallow small sandy beach, away from prying eyes. Mesmerized when she took the rest of her bathing suit off and plunged straight into the water, swimming towards his kayak, she flipped it before he could react, and he was suddenly in the water with her. She was laughing like a young girl, so glad about her prank. And he was laughing as well. It was a moment of intense pleasure. She could generate these. She did it without knowing. She did it by gathering all the energies, the vibrations, the elements that surrounded her, and after absorbing all of them, sending them back. He received her and the salted sea all at once. Her mouth on his, her nakedness against his skin.

The sun was still warm. His kayak drifted to the beach, rolling gently in the waves. The scent of pine trees lingering longer on this side of the cliff, the sound of distant bells chiming as the goats went about unaware. The young man, on the other hand, was aware of it all. His mind responded to the surroundings just as it always did with objects—responding to every detail, every offered gift.

THE THIRD NIGHT WAS HERS, AS PLANNED. Adam had the next one. She had hinted that she also wanted the last one, and he'd been happy to agree. He was lucky to have a woman who actually thought like him—or at least appeared to see and explore his point of view: that if it was shared and if it was done in love and trust, there was power in those escapades—the power to live intense moments and create striking memories.

She had told him to wear relaxed clothes. He had biked and swum, and then swum again, rotating his shoulders underwater, improving his backstroke; the sea penetrating his nose, his mouth, the space between his teeth, the back of his throat, and awakening his skin, stinging the thin scratches.

As he swam, each stroke awoke another glimpse of the incredible red night they had lived. In the waves, he saw, once again, everyone dancing and moving, moving into each other under the same rhythm, the same red aura, same red *chakra.* In his mind he was hanging on to some of the previous night's memories a little longer; like the rock candy melting ever slowly within the confines of his mouth. At exactly 4:00 AM, the DJ stopped the music. The white-suited woman had emptied the room, and at once all had been gone. Layla kissed him good-night and left.

He had suddenly felt exhausted without her and had gone for a walk through the sleepy town. His steps brought him behind a street corner to a tiny bakery that opened just before sunrise. There, he bought a sweet pastry wrapped in perfect dough. When he turned around, he saw, looking at him with a subtle smile, the girl who had given him the massage the night before—an eternity by then. He had been stunned—she was exquisitely beautiful, even at the break of dawn. Especially at that hour. He'd taken her to a terrace overlooking the sea, already alive with the faintest glow of early light, and shared the pastry with her.

What had she been listening to? he'd asked, pointing to the earphones.

"Klaus Nomi," she'd answered, taking out one her earbuds, and placed it in his ear. She'd hit play and the song flooded them together.

"Come to the beach with me," he had said in a tone at once commanding and inquisitive.

"Yes," she'd answered, still looking out in the distance.

She had hopped on the back of his scooter, hips straddling the vibrating seat, arms tight around him in the early chill. They'd become one unit that flowed down towards the sea, as everything there did—even St. John the Divine must have soaked his soul into the salt of the bay waters. They'd passed the spot where she first saw him in the open car. She'd thought of it and squeezed herself even tighter to him, feeling his firm ass within the width of her femininity.

"The water is too cold," she had said.

He'd smiled at her, then dove right in. "Come on, darling," he'd assured her, "It will only be cold for a second."

He'd been right. It always got warmer once you moved into the water, yet there was always that fatal one second of time that kept most on the edge forever.

Her feet were in the water. Her knees. The top of her thighs.

"Come on," he urged her over, his hair slicked back by the still dark sea. "Come *on*, baby." He could see her silhouette against the distant mountain, her head obscuring the monastery and Hora. Her legs, slightly parted, let a ray of moonlight stream beneath her. He could feel the magnetic pull of her pussy. It was hovering just above the water. Duplicated by reflection. Multiplied in his mind.

She dove in, splitting the calm surface with her outstretched arms and the dark strands of her hair—her face embracing the cold. He'd caught her as soon as she surfaced, caught her from behind and stood behind her, his hands on her breasts. The sea had just been waking up, capturing the gold and crimson of first sunlight. They had stood there together, warming up the world around them.

"RELAXED CLOTHES" WAS ALL LAYLA HAD SAID. He found long gray cotton pants in the back of the closet, and with them wore a pale blue T-shirt, washed countless times and now softer than air. He recognized the smell as he walked down the steps towards his nocturnal destiny.

"I love that!" he said, pointing to the thin crusted pizzas. She had set a wood-burning stove in the garden, and with a wave of her hand, an older Italian man brought them the small pizzas. "Fresh tomatoes and the best mozzarella," she said. And then there were some with *bottarga* and artichokes, and also some surprising ones sweetened by local figs.

Their backs propped up by pillows, his eyes moved from one wall to the next. A different black-and-white movie was projected on each one, shining bright even on the ceiling. It was pure genius! he thought, each surface showing its own movie. He recognized a few. *Jules et Jim. My Night at Maud's.* Those were always her favorites, but also *La Dolce Vita* and *Roman Holiday.* The sound would originate from one movie scene at a time only, and sometimes all the walls' images merged into one movie and the same scene overflowed the entire room.

"Movie night!" he said, with the biggest smile. "I love it. Thank you, sweetheart!"

They ate their pizzas while watching the movies and cuddled together. She drank the local white wine, and he drank tequila on the rocks. Now and then, a scene from a color movie would reveal itself. He saw the Malaparte House in Godard's movie with Brigitte Bardot.

"Brigitte Bardot, Bardot!" he sang out loud and they both laughed at the mention of that song that always reminded them of their daughter. She wanted to say "I miss her," but she knew not to. He looked at her with added love and started kissing her—her body, her taste, familiar and intoxicating. She pressed a button on the remote. Gone were the old movies, and in their place, he saw the unmistakable flesh and skin of porn. Multiple screens, multiple choices. His eyes swimming from one wall to the next.

"We can change it," she said with a broad smile, pulling out a small digital screen from beneath her pillow, "We can pick what you want."

"You know what I want," he answered. "I want whatever it is you like." She laughed almost awkwardly. They both knew what she liked to watch.

He became big in her mouth. She loved the feeling of almost suffocating under him. Her legs were apart, and his tongue had brought her over the edge already. He licked her, letting her juices and his saliva run along the deeper crevice, and she felt the glass dildo slip smoothly into her, the pink glass flower resting flush against her bleached ass. He came back to her, face to face. They kissed each other, tasting each other all at once. She loved the fullness in her ass and how he held her so tight.

"Come!" she said. "Come, please. I beg you," she added.

He made sure that his hardness found her slowly, ever so slowly, so she could feel how big he was. For her. Only for her. And then he took her faster, feeling the presence of the glass as he sank deep into her and flipped her over as all the walls echoed all around them. Scenes of dual pleasure. Double trouble.

"Did you bring the small black one?" she asked.

"Yes," he laughed, and pulled out the toy from the pocket of his tossed pants. It was short and had a counterweight within it. She felt him, found him with eyes closed, and made sure the small plug went in easily. She went on all fours in front of him, and he watched the pink glass from her offered ass reflect the light from all the screens. He smiled. He could almost make out the movies themselves in the raised glass petals, all variations of the same scene: two men simultaneously possessing the same woman. He knew she had anticipated it. The men and women were all good-looking. That was always her prerequisite.

She was watching the screens. Her hand slipped under her

as she found herself. The sight was astonishing to him. Never would a rock candy-sucking youngster ever imagine that women would allow such a thing, let alone enjoy it. And on screen, and on the bed, they all seemed to love it. And hard as a bull, he went in her. He felt the little ball move within his core as he reached a certain rhythm. And she loved that rhythm. It was fast and free. He slapped her ass. And again. And faster, and faster. She arched her back, and he grabbed her long hair and went faster and deeper again. She clicked the movies off with one touch of her finger, and just like that, they were alone again—no one to have to talk to or say goodbye to.

Moments later, they were sleeping deeply in each other's arms.

THE VISITING CURATOR WAS FRENCH, with Russian origins. He had grown up familiar with Catholic images and Russian Orthodox icons. He had always been fascinated by the attempts at religious imagery. Thank goodness for those attempts, he thought. Without them, there might forever have been no trace of an artistic creation.

The Church and Royalty—they were the two providers for the only art that persisted. Perhaps, because art was no longer dependent on the kings and queens, or the priests and cardinals, these same authorities had lost power over time. The ubiquitous ease with which humans could express themselves artistically nowadays had uprooted the dominance of these ancient monopolies.

He was sought after because of his extensive knowledge of different iconographies. He could expertly cross-reference creeds and churches. Just then, though, he had only one church in his mind, and that was the temple of her body. Of Layla and the beauty of her curves, the elegance of her posture, the invitation of her altar. Yesterday, on the isolated sandy beach, she had let him play with her and made him cum into the sea, like Kronos. But she had not let him enter her. "I am married," she had told him. "Only my husband can allow it."

All day today he had been stuck deep in underground rooms and vaults, holding up hidden secret treasures, filling his being with devotional artifacts and magical objects that sometimes, somehow, opened portals. Certain days can have that special power as well. Apparently, on this particular one in August, there was to be a psychic lion-portal opening. He had seen it on a post and paid little attention. However, it felt as if his entire being *was* being opened by this woman. His mind, his body, his soul had been aching for her and her scent, the taste of her intimacy. He'd brought his hand back to his face in vain. All scent of her had vanished into the wood of the sculptures, and he'd smiled at the thought that they were the perfect vehicle for her realized desires.

By the time he made it to the beach, he was told that she had left already. Upset and dejected, he'd gone for a long swim. He took stroke after stroke, moving the water beneath him as if he was rotating the mass of the earth itself. He swam until he wanted no more. As he looked up, he noticed that he was close to the sandy beach from the day before. He swam to it. He climbed onto the sand, looking for traces of their adventure, and found none. Nature, as it always does, had cleaned up everything. He had lain down naked, feeling the weight of the still blue sky. With his eyes closed, his hand found and molded his dreams. Once satisfied he swam back and went for lunch.

EARLIER THE SAME DAY, SHE'D HAD HER BREAKFAST in the usual spot by the eucalyptus tree in her garden, close to a tall, remarkable plant with large green velvety leaves that looked like human hands. On the leaves were thin ridges that mimicked blood vessels, as if it were a plant born from the seed of men within the fertile soil of the island. She had been fascinated by that plant and had even taken pictures of herself naked among the various leaves, the giant hands aspiring to touch her.

The Greek coffee was strong. She sipped it slowly thinking about what she wanted to do that day. She did not want to stay there and get in the way of Adam's preparation for the upcoming night. She went to the beach instead. She had wanted to see the young man with his cigar and his long, big cock. Not because of it but because he was the perfect foil for her current state of mind. Although she barely knew him and it was strange and unusual that she was so intimate with him, he felt like the right antidote to all the decadence she was willing to do then— a day companion while Adam remained her man of night.

But he had not been at the beach, and she'd left early, knowing that, by leaving, she was going to miss him. She was a little disappointed yet felt the need to go. Sometimes she followed impulses that made no immediate sense.

On the way home, she'd had a late lunch in Hora with some friends. The cold beer she drank straight from the bottle, and the flavor of the pure white fish topped by deep green olive oil, coalesced exquisitely. It was the quality of the products that made it so. That guy too was quality, she thought to herself. She looked up—and much to her surprise, there he was, watching her from another table, sitting alone. She smiled, grateful for fate. In French they use the word *reconnaissant* for gratefulness. It literally means "to recognize" or "to know once again."

She had left money with her girlfriends and left the restaurant. Discreetly, he followed her. They walked a few steps away from each other for a short while. He followed her higher and higher in Hora, watching every step she took, until they reached the top esplanade before the monastery. They were alone up there. He leaned slowly towards the mouth he desired so much and kissed it, tenderly locking his lips to hers. Until his tongue could hold no more and with his whole being, he found her.

She let herself go—swimming in his water now.

He led her by the hand through a private door to the monastery, up the stairs and, unseen by all, into his room. The late day light streamed through a narrow opening and at that moment lit the porcelain sculpture he had placed on the high ledge, against the wall. She let him devour her, looking up and smiling when she saw the face of the delicate cherub light up in the ray of light. She let herself cum under his tongue, and then she tasted him deep in her mouth— her throat a heaven for him.

Later she took her phone out and asked if she could take a few pictures. Still enthralled, he acquiesced. She shot him naked, outside, sitting on top of the stonewall, the smoke of his cigar dispersing into the sunset clouds. Beneath his relaxed body existed a vaulted building of religious conventions, above him the wide-open sky.

She was satisfied with the pictures.

It was almost time for her to meet Adam for the fourth night. This was his last one to orchestrate.

She was getting ready for the "rendezvous" as he had requested. *Rendezvous.* That meant an appointment, a date of sorts, a meeting, but in French it also meant "to surrender." She was ready. She would go.

Under a dark green silk gown she was wearing the latex undergarment he had asked for. It was strange walking in it. It rubbed, it squeaked, it impaired her. She kind of liked it, which surprised her. How had he come up with it? she wondered.

She reached the second-floor antechamber, now filled with fragrant white flowers, and was immediately surrounded by a cloud of pungent scents. She opened the bedroom door. It was a shock. There was no structure left to the bedroom. He'd had all furniture removed and, in their place, had created an inner garden. Soil was heaped thigh-high on one side of the room, in a semicircle supported by planks of dark wood. In the moist, balmy soil, he had arranged for the plants to be transferred from the garden. Even the tall ones with the velvet-like hands, and smaller ones that reflected light on their shiny leaves and spread themselves along contorted stems— each rich with green life and luscious textures. Each fragrant. She inhaled the deep, intoxicating scent of the crazy mix of plants and flowers and was swept over.

The latex made sense now, like rubber running from a caoutchouc tree, like original sap that flushed through her body and laced her up.

He called for her from the mattress, lying right on the floor facing the empty white walls. She could hear the music that drifted through the embedded speakers in the soil, a recording of the DJ's remix session. It carried echoes of red color right through the green foliage and resonated deep in her brain. She knew he was ready to please her—blissfully unaware that, moments before, she had reached the same heights over and over with the other man. Very gently, he took her green gown off and she spread herself for him. He leaned forward and in turn inhaled her, and the plants, and the flowers. He took it all in—the mixed scents, but also the touch of synthetic rubber and its unnatural sound, like dry fingers rubbing themselves in slow, slow motion.

The music flowed through their bodies, pulsing in the veins of the mystical plant. Her hips swayed in a primitive dance. Once again, she let her body go. She was present at the "rendezvous." If anything, the orgasm from earlier made her even more receptive. He found her fantastic, erotic and extraordinary. He kept his face in her. Touching and feeling the layer of latex that transformed her into a robot-like fixture.

She played the part. She let him explore. She let him be, and he became. He gathered the powers that surrounded them, and he blossomed all over her. Blossomed over her naked breast and the curve of her soft belly and the abyss of initial sin.

She was naked and dressed and transparent all at once. Becoming the Original Woman all over again for him. All for him. All in the ecstasy of the moment.

She finally looked to the side. Next to the fire that he had started earlier was the massage girl sitting on black high heels and wearing tight black garters and nothing else. She was uncomfortable. She was hot and glowing from sweat. She did not move. She was obedient.

Layla smiled. Now she knew where this could lead. Her husband must have really liked the girl to bring her back again. She was pleased. After all, it had been her choice initially. Her own doing.

He nodded, signaling for the girl to get up. She did.

With his fingers, he beckoned her to twirl.

She did, revealing in the glow of the fire the luminance of her curves, her shapely long legs and tight ass—all of her nakedness.

She was cartoon perfect.

She wanted more. More than just modeling her groomed body. She wanted them to seduce her, to abuse her.

Layla read it, and she stood up and went to kiss her. Tongue against tongue.

Black silk against milk latex, their legs finding each other, skin soft as they rubbed against each other. The girl's beads of sweat trickled down her back, hot and slippery under Layla's fingers. She caressed her, letting her hand mix the salt of wet skin with the sweet juices of her being.

The scent of the earth was overwhelming.

Layla knew what to do next. She had seen them nailed onto the wall as she entered the room. She strapped the girl to the wall with the thick black leather cuffs, securing her arms up and to the side and legs apart, in a perfect letter X. Like a painting by Wade Guyton.

He drank from his glass of mezcal as she was being tied up, admiring the new black and white shape she made in the green room. The fire was smoldering, and the candles were burning wax at their own speed, each on their own, like the girl. He played with her. With the handle of the whip, stiff between her legs, he touched her. She was dripping wet. His wife went to her, touched her with fingers that spelled lust. The whip went, finding both at times. He slapped their backs and thighs, moving with the music, their moans fusing in the thick air, fueling his swings.

The room became even hotter. The scent of the plants, of the moist earth and the women linked together was intoxicating. He took his shirt off. He reached for one of the candles and, ever so slowly, dripped the hot wax over the bound body of the girl. She moaned, her body alive with pain and pleasure. She looked at him, asking for more with her eyes. He found another wet candle.

Layla whispered to him over the pulse of the beat, and he complied. He whipped. He kissed. He burned. He found.

Before he released her and took her, he drew, with a soft piece of cold black coal, her bound outline on the white wall.

IN ANCIENT MYTHOLOGY, THE NYMPH ECHO GOT punished by her mistress, Hera, for having colluded to distract her by speech while Zeus, Hera's husband, was fooling around. Echo was therefore destined to repeat from there on the last words of a sentence only. She took refuge in the forest and fell in love with the handsome Narcissus. Unfortunately, Narcissus, enamored only with his own visual reflection, rejected the beautiful Echo. He did not care for the constant repetition, the reflection of his own words, that gentle Echo could offer. Despondent, she hid deeper and deeper, surviving only in the caves and grottos and canyons. It is only in these isolated places that anyone can connect with her now.

THIS WAS TO BE THEIR FINAL DAY, their final night. She had the room whitewashed but kept the charcoal drawing of the girl's submission. She knew that Adam was probably with her that morning. It did bother her a little, but then again, she had the curator to contend with—and to be content with. She smiled. Soon she and Adam would be back home together, and she was almost ready for it. There was one more night left. She had already laid out the plans for it. For the rest of the day, she was free.

She decided to go back to the sea for another swim. She parked above the twin beaches.

Her husband was there. He was actually alone. She had been wrong. She was happy about that. The whole week had been crazy and so different from who they were. She was worried at times that they would lose each other within all this decadence. Yet she could not remember loving her husband more than she did as she walked towards him, and he waved to her.

They swam together. He moved around her like a dolphin, swimming circles, his head back and laughing out loud above the clear waters.

He dove under her. From below, he saw her sunlit shape against the surface. He went deeper, where the water gets almost as dark as night. He had no fear. He was focused. On her. On the image of that loving shape that waited for him expectantly, unafraid. She knew he always came back to her, was always there.

His face emerged close to hers. She looked into his blue eyes. She sent her love on the bouncing surface of the clear sea, and he embraced it. Smiling even wider to himself as he reached into the side of his tight bathing shorts she loved to hate so much and prepared his surprise. He distracted her just long enough to slip it in his mouth and then took her hand to his lips and fed her fingers in. In it she found the coils of a metallic chain and she started pulling on it. A succession of brilliant stones arose from him like a green garland. It was the marvelous bracelet of emeralds she had recently pointed out to him in a store back home. She was stunned. They swam back to shore and fell on the warm towels and spread their bodies under the sun and the incoming waves and whatever the next stars would bring.

She was in charge that last night. It was her wish to please him completely, and she reckoned she knew how to do it. She had thought about it a lot. How she wanted to combine her impulse and her love, the vision and the flesh of it. How she thought she read her husband well. How she was willing to take a chance but not go beyond the point of no return. And that was almost as scary as the anticipation was exciting. She was shivering at the thought of it, and then she knew she had to let go, or nothing would happen at all. She reached for the new bracelet strapped around her slender wrist and let the green stones speak to her.

On this last night they were going to meet even later than usual. The sky became as dark as the deep waters—Aphrodite spying on them from the distant glow of Venus. The air in the house was still reminiscent of the scent of wet earth and plants from the previous night. Windows were open on his top floor, and the cross-ventilation caused a gentle breeze.

He let the alcohol and the winds mix. Engrossed in a poem about love by Cavafy, he caressed his chest without even noticing it. Over the years his nipples had become erogenous. It had not always been that way. To him, this was a blessing. Whenever his wife touched him there, whenever she squeezed him, he would be driven into focusing all his attention back on the realm of pure physicality, away from all the words and worlds floating in his mind. He would become even more engorged. And she liked that. She liked him harder.

At the agreed time, he walked into the room. He wore a pale blue pareo draped around his narrow hips and an open, white shirt wrapped around his tanned swimmer's shoulders. He was barefoot on the still-warm floor. He noted that the room had been whitewashed all over again. The large bed was elevated on a platform, which was the way she liked her beds. There was a mirror on the right-side wall facing the bed, and on the wall she had kept the drawn outline of the bound woman. All traces of cuffs had been removed. The room felt austere, almost monastic. The only indulgence to vanity were the leaning mirror and the charcoal drawing.

Earlier, she had been listening to the Thievery Corporation. As he was reading, he had recognized their favorite songs, but then she had switched to the "Red Party" soundtrack. That playlist had become the musical identity of this house and time.

She was dressed all in white. A simple linen summer dress that opened in front with unusually large red plastic buttons. The red buttons should have alerted him of what was going to happen, but he was just engrossed in looking at her and her beauty. She had a tiny black thong under the thin white fabric of the dress. He could guess it was there but could barely see it. It was a masquerade of an undergarment, really, both revealing and inviting. It was just how he liked it. The outfit was to be his gift, he figured.

She wore his most recent gift on her left wrist.

At the base of the fireplace she had set up a bottle of tequila, some ice in a silver bucket, and a bottle of rosé for her-self in another silver bucket. He drank from a thick, multi-faceted glass tumbler. It was a glass from back home, he realized. He smiled as she gave him the drink.

"You think ahead," he said.

"Yes. Always."

It was a small memento, but he could feel himself being back home for an instant. In his mind, he saw the paintings and the photograph collection. Men are more visual, it is said. They respond to images, to visions. And she always made sure that he had plenty of them to fill his head.

"So happy it is you and me," he said.

"Yes," she answered quietly, avoiding his gaze. She bent over and reached for a black camera case. "I brought your camera too," she said.

"I see. You really came well prepared."

"Yes, I know how much you like taking pictures." She smiled. "Go ahead to your heart's content tonight. If you want," she added with a seductive whisper, perfectly covering her nervousness.

He checked the camera. The battery was fully charged, and it had a new digital card in place. She did things right, he thought, and he started taking a few pictures to check the light. These new cameras were equipped with a digital light-enhancement device, so he could capture her even in candle- and moonlight. He liked that combination of dim sources of light— one man made, one stellar, both natural.

She glowed in the screen, her skin a hazy delight as she stripped slowly for him and the camera. He shot the white curtains that floated in the open window air and the white dress as she undid the buttons one by one and let it slide to the floor. She was oiled. She was perfect. He desired her so much—her moves, her sensuality.

The pareo had been a good idea. Soon he would slip it off, and let it fall, and take her, all the while filming her long legs and the exquisite darkness of the triangle she still wore. His hips were moving gently with the music. On the camera screen, he saw her bite her lower lip and stare at the main door. He had no idea how terrified she was at that instant. She could hardly stand anymore, and she sat at the edge of the bed, legs together, facing the massive door. In her mind, she imagined that it opened by itself, and flowing away from it was a narrow stretch of open road. She could either escape on it, or she could wait and let events unfold even further into the room. Into her.

On cue, the short haired woman in the white suit opened the door from the outside and ushered in a young man. He wore dark blue pants and a white cotton shirt, just like the men from the red party. The young man looked at Layla with a giant smile on his face. She did not move; his smile froze. He saw the other man in the room. This must be her husband, he thought.

Both men looked at each other in silence for a short period. She was still biting her lower lip as she stood up, looking imploringly towards Adam, unsure if what she had planned was what he truly wanted. He had spoken about this countless times in the past, yet, right now, that felt so far away and so long ago now, just whims uttered during the throes of passion in a city way beyond here. What was unfolding now was real. They were all physically in the same room. Flesh to feel. Flesh to hold. Flesh to play with. To suck. Maybe to fuck.

As she saw him bring the camera back to his eye, she finally released her lip and walked to the young man. Still quivering, she smiled at him and said, "It's okay," and then took his hand and brought him closer to the bed. She sat once again at the edge, looked up again, somewhere between apologetically and hopefully, at her husband. He had shifted position in order to get better light, his shadow away from them now. She faced the young man's dark blue pants and proceeded to nervously unbutton the fabric. He was big. Once again, she took him in her mouth. Not too far this time. It was too soon. She held him with her linked fingers, the emerald bracelet shining in the light. Then she stopped. She wanted him to last longer and go all the way. She had made up her mind. It was too late to go back.

Adam was initially capturing their reflection in the mirror, as if he could not absorb the reality of it all yet. But soon he could resist no longer, and he started moving around them, as they lay down on the white sheets—witnessing it all unfold on the digital screen. He saw her slip her thong to the side, take the young man's cock with her other hand, and place it on the wetness of her open pussy. She kept her thigh wide open to the side so that Adam had more light for his camera, the candles on the platform revealing the full impact of their shared infidelity.

The young man was moving faster now. The beat of the music took on a new meaning. He was ravishing her, and she started to moan. Adam could see she was looking for him, so he pointed the camera directly to her face. She still had a quizzical look, but he put the camera aside and smiled at her, smiled with a sweetness she recognized, and then she let her head go back.

His camera capturing her exposed neck, her naked skin, her spread legs. As he got closer and closer, he took in the full girth of the man as it penetrated her.

She whispered to the young man to cum on her. And as such she was warning Adam. She could feel it building up within her. He captured the semen as it came alive, exploding in arcs over her belly, spilling on her chest and on her still-raw lower lip, bruised from where she had bitten it earlier.

He watched it, and somehow it felt as if he was in a dream. They had spoken about it in the past as a fantasy, and now she had actually done it—for him, for his sake. He knew that.

And now, all he wanted was to thank her.

The young man rolled over, still panting. She moved to the side, retrieved a fragrant, warm, wet towel from a bamboo container at the bedside and cleaned herself up with it, swallowing the splashes that had reached her lips.

"Boy, you were well prepared!" he laughed as he removed his pareo. He no longer saw the other body as he took her now fully naked pussy. They made love. She made him even bigger as she reached up and squeezed.

"Did you come?" he asked in a breath.

"No. Only you."

He flipped her sideways and, still penetrating her all the while, brought her on top of him. Her hips moving, she started dancing on him. He grabbed her ass with both hands and pinned her down deep as he kept moving in and out of her. Then gently, with a firm hand on her back, he guided her body closer to his, her breasts against his chest. His hands spread her open. In the mirror he saw what he expected. The young man licked her at first and then, with his cock swollen again, he took her from behind, letting his hips fully meet hers. She moved with the ecstasy of one surrendering to weightlessness and overwhelming bliss. The sacredness of the moment did not escape him. He kept the camera rolling as their mixed moans reached the music of heavenly delight.

At that same instant, in the monastery, it was time for morning chants. The priests were singing. A few isolated nuns were chanting, and all the combined voices from house and church linked into an ethereal chorus that welcomed the early morning light.

The young man was down on one side of the bed, dazed and asleep, dreaming of fantastic and unbelievable ecstasy.

Husband and wife smiled at each other. They knew they had done good for all the expecting souls. They got up from the bed together.

Epilogue

IT WAS NOT THE RISING SUN THAT WOKE up the young man. It was the vibration of moving rotors that filled the room—a thunderous noise that made the curtains billow. He stood up and, still fastening his pants, climbed to the top terrace of the house. He immediately realized that she was in that helicopter, lifting away from the island. He looked up and put both hands on the back of his head—a farewell as much as a realization that they were gone. He lay back on the wide outdoor mattress, his body spread out as he looked at birds flying back and forth. A pearl-gray dove landed close by. They looked at each other.

Down below, the dark-haired woman went back into the main bedroom, still resonating with the scents and emotions of the most recent sex. She looked at the drawn outline of what had been her bound body—grateful that Layla had left it for her, almost like a Cycladic icon. She instinctively took off the white suit and then, with a thoughtful finger, caressed the part where her drawn legs met. It made her wet. She walked closer to the wall and laid her frame back in the primal shape, her cheek against the warm white plaster, inhaling the scent of her past pleasure.

In the distance, she heard the blades of the helicopter fading away.

PEONIES

O N ONE SIDE OF THE HOTEL LOBBY SAT a free-standing wooden table with a large, beautiful vase that contained flowers tightly packed together. Dark pink, almost red, they were silent spheres ready to explode in bloom. With petals still tight, stems full and solid, the peonies greeted the guests of Le Meurice with a blast of mystery for those who cared to look their way. You could miss them in the rush of the day. You could mistake them for fake decoration. But if you paid attention, they gave it back to you. Who'd put them there? A man? A woman? Probably someone in the early hours, while the patrons slept. Someone who, slowly, flower by flower, gathered them in a single vase of translucent glass for all to witness their full splendor.

It was a wedding that brought us there, a still unmarried

couple from New York City. Weddings can be a little tough, sometimes awkward, when you go together and are not yet married, but we knew where we stood on the ladder of expectations. Sure, there would be tears gathering in her eyes when the ceremony unfolded, but they would be for the couple, not for herself. Or at least that's what I told myself. She did have a tendency to cry at schmaltzy moments in movies. I would glance at her, and she would shield her damp, big brown eyes with her hand. I loved her for that. It made me laugh. And she would then nudge me away, tenderly, ashamed of her girlishness.

Paris is a good place to cry. Paris, and Venice, and maybe a Mediterranean island.

The hotel allegedly served as headquarters to the Nazis during the occupation of Paris. That titbit had kept me away from the five-star palace forever, but, following yet another renovation and with the wedding party congregating there, it made sense to give in and spend a few nights. After all, that may be the best revenge—to go back and live fabulously where pain and deceit were prevalent eighty years before. As it is said, "Living well is the best revenge."

What did "well" mean? Had I done a good enough job? Time itself was running out to tell. I was entering decades that had seemed so distant a lifelong before. There was no time in everyday life to really reflect upon it. She was young. She needed attention, and I wanted hers, like a glass of water in the morning sun. Like the flowers in the hotel lobby.

Daytime events unfolded with an aura of predictability, filled with art and art people and planned luxury. Moments slid into each other seamlessly, from museums to galleries, from bookstores to clothing stores. We met sunsets with cocktails in ornate rooms and then moved together on the dance floor, moving faster as the music grew wilder. We had fun together. We were a unit, a couple. People looked at our love and smiled.

Nighttimes were different, for we had agreed that they belonged to me alone. It was her gift to me—one I could enjoy as I wished.

And I knew what that was. I wanted to go to what we called "The Club" in the midst of our lovemaking back home, when I whispered to her all the things I would do to her when we got there, in front of prying eyes and hungry hands. It could only exist in Paris and lived on class and expectations, lingerie and fantasies, darkness and nakedness. It was run by a woman, and the madame at the door only allowed in those she thought appropriate. They, in turn, were expected to behave with the politeness such a place commands. High heels and naked legs were de rigueur—"*sex oblige.*" She knew this and, on this trip, had travelled with all the prerequisite accoutrements and more. She was not sure why, really. Maybe it was because I so very much seemed to like watching her get ready. That night, though, in the comfort of our hotel room with its inviting oversized bed, she asked me in a doubtful tone, "Do we really have to go tonight?"

"Yes! We have to, darling. After all, you're all dressed up, or down. And we *are* in Paris for just a couple nights. . . let's go." I made sure the determination was clear in my hopeful voice.

"But I just like the *fantasy* of it all."

"I know, baby," I sweet-talked her. "But there is no fantasy without a bit of reality in it." I knew this could oscillate the other way, and we could remain in our room, mimicking the countless nights of couples before us.

Ecstasy is an individual perception. It is qualified in general terms, in an all-encompassing definition that seems to require no explanation, yet it remains different from one person to another. Each opens up to it in their own way, a bit like the peonies that open up hour by hour in their vase. "In Chinese paintings," I tell her as we pass the vase in the lobby, "an open peony on the canvas is a sign that the woman portrayed is open to sexual advances."

She barely acknowledges me. *"This peony is pretty damn closed for now."*

The night was darker on Rue de Rivoli since the city mayor had stopped all car traffic there a few months earlier, pushing the buildings surrounding them into shadows in the so-called City of Lights. It was late and the usually busy arcades were empty of people. Along the mosaics of the sidewalk, the ghostly imprint of thousands of feet remained, though. I was not thinking about those people; instead I was thinking about the few that gathered in the club every night of the week, like bees attracted to the pollen of a bright pistil. As much as the bee needed to plunge deep in the open crown of the flowers in order to survive, no one needed to be in that place and at that time. And yet they came, walking in couples, hand-in-hand, gathering for the nightly bacchanal.

The sound of her heels resonated as a faint echo under the arches of the street before we made a left, away from the Louvre and all its marvels and towards the steps we would take if we were selected and ushered in.

She wore the see-through lingerie she had picked up for this occasion some time before, at a moment when she was in the mood. It was sophisticated and sexy when she tried it on at home.

"Vulgar and too calculated" is what she saw when she examined her reflection in a mirror by the bar.

I loved it. The black lace spoke volumes of the bondage of my desires, and my hand stayed on her ass as I watched women and men checking her see-through gown, observing the intricate pattern it created on her laced-up skin. Her breasts were partly hidden but not her shapely ass. It was totally in the flavor of France, where butts and legs take precedence over the venerated bosom on the young continent of the U.S.A.

I loved watching my hand slowly outline the curve of

her delicious shape. I loved the furtive glances I could catch in the mirror as people debated whether she was a wife or a whore. All the while, the tequila, cooled by the wide ice cubes, found its way down my throat. In the rooms behind us, strangers also found their way down lips and throats. You could sense it. Even if you could not see it from the room we were standing in, it was palpable in the air, like a flow of heavy oxygen that carried the scent of fully bloomed flowers. It was as if we were part of a giant orchestra, with the strings in the front room we were in and the more primitive drums and horns in the back.

The back rooms were where the musical score really opened up and where the music poured out in pulsing primal waves. There, a voluptuous woman who had danced so provocatively on the small disco floor moments earlier was now crouched on the thickness of her mate. She was offering her exposed ass to whoever wanted to touch it, and her body beckoned for more as she grabbed exploring hands and guided them to the hidden. Lying on the velvet sofa close to her, an elegant woman barely clad in an outfit made of black silk flowers had pushed the top aside revealing the beauty of her breasts just as her legs slipped out of the many slits of her dress. Everywhere, lust was happening. On the side sofa, two other women kissed and gradually disrobed each other under the stares of their men. The crowd gathered around them.

Nature was taking over. The waves from many seas were

filling up the subterrain cave as if it were a deep grotto on the coast of a Mediterranean island. It was a dance, and my eyes caught it all.

To be able to read the moment, to understand its emotion, requires a certain mindset. Much to my chagrin, she was not in the mood, and she never entered the grotto, and instead stayed emotionally disconnected, as if on a pier watching a slow boat float away. I understood, and it hurt.

That is perhaps the least desirable feeling for a couple in love—for there is no pleasure without the pleasure of the other.

So we left.

THE NEXT DAY WAS THE WEDDING. It was very special and different and filled with fashionable people. The women were dressed as vividly as the other women in the club had been un-dressed, and they looked particularly beautiful. Their dresses had the splendor of sacred objects that had been carefully un-wrapped from suitcases flown in from all over the world. I watched them as the Parisian sun stood out late, solid in its light, and as the dresses twirled, while the tequila drifted in my veins drop by drop.

She was wearing a dark, tight, form-fitting dress with pur-ple blooms embossed all over. Open blooms, I reflected with a smile. The club was no longer a concern for me—the trip was over and done with. I figured I could live vicariously through the images captured the night before. Which is fine, I thought again. "Totally fine," I heard myself say out loud.

"What are you saying?" she asked.

"Nothing, dear. You look beautiful tonight," I told her. That compliment reminded me of one of my favorite Eric Clapton songs, when the singer watches his wife get ready for the night and compliments her on her looks. And then she has to carry him home at the end of the party, I recalled as well, with a smile. "You are the most beautiful one here tonight," I added.

"Come on!" she retorted with a laugh. "There's the bride." She pointed. "Look, she is *marvelous!*"

"Yes, she is indeed, but to me you're the most beautiful one."

MUCH LATER THAT EVENING, I REPEATED the sentence, whispering it into her ear as she laid her head against my shoulder, deep in the cozy recess of the cave at the club. She was naked except for her heels.

"Always leave the party when it is at its best," my father always said, and she agreed to leave when I told her it was time to go.

"But I want to go to the club next," she had said. "And I want to go dressed like this. No going back to the hotel room to change."

"They may not let us in," I warned her, though I was pleasantly surprised.

"*Tant pis!*" she answered with a shrug and a wave of her hand.

HER EYES WERE GLISTENING IN THE DIM LIGHT of the dance floor, and glistening again when she pulled her dress over her head in the mellow darkness of the room. She was already completely naked under it, her panties safe in my pocket after she removed them in the Uber on the way there. What a laugh we had in the back of the car as I kissed her neck and naked shoulders! I kissed them again as she picked a stranger in the darkness. The man stood behind her and caressed her body, his hands like a layer of clothing along her waist, her ass, her back. I looked up. Even in the darkness, even within the haze of the tequila, I could see that he had entered her. Her ass pressed against him, and his hands moved to open her up some more. He was flowing in her now, back and forth. I could see the connection now, the link of flesh between them, and I was still mesmerized by it when I felt her body sink down further and her mouth engulf me and move in the same rhythm she was getting danced on.

She may have to walk *me* home tonight, I thought through the vapors of my euphoria.

The ecstasy was real. Back in the hotel lobby, the flowers had opened, releasing all their scent and color. I could feel them from where I was standing. I'd felt it all along—the petals opening up one by one. "Like the rose petals in *Beauty and the Beast*," I told her.

"You are a beast indeed," she replied as we walked around the club one last time, among outstretched hands that caressed her like the low leaves of trees had caressed me in my morning run. Like love, caressing us all the way back to sleep in each other's arms in the hotel room that had once, years before, known a different fate.

QUATTUOR

DAY

Maid

INKPUSSY18, SHE TYPED—HER USERNAME—and, within moments, she was listening to her kind of techno music. It was just before sunrise. Others were listening as well. She could see the comments scrolling continuously down the screen. They were all partying in private by then. It was the end of their night. It was the beginning of her day. The sun was about to rise.

Everyone can see the sunset. Sunrises, on the other hand, require a certain set of sacrifices, she thought. She was getting ready to go to work. It was not supposed to happen this way, but the world, and the distorted biology of nature, had decided differently. She had started an internship six weeks ago for her

Ecole d'Hôtellerie: It was meant to provide future hotel managers with a personal understanding of the underbelly of the hotel world. Usually three to four weeks long, the internship entailed working at one of the essential jobs of the industry—like doorman, or bellhop, or waiter. She had picked a housekeeping role, not because she really wanted the experience, but because it was the only job available in the hotel she wanted to go to. It was on a Mediterranean island, which, as a girl living in Oslo, was irresistible to her. And now that no one could travel any longer, she had chosen to stay on the island a little longer. She had accepted the offer of the manager and stayed on as a paid employee. He needed all the help he could get. Her only request had been to work on the top floor. He had accepted. The fifth floor, the top one, was also the club floor. It was half-full then and therefore provided her with extra free time during the day.

She was walking towards the hotel. The wind seemed a little stronger than usual today. She listened for a moment to the whispers in the trees, and then, nonchalantly, put on her air pods and let the music flood her. She was walking quickly on a winding, well-worn path that flanked the hills. To her left was the sea. She could not see the sun yet, it was hiding behind a smaller island, but the sky had brightened, and the path was clear.

She had the stride of an athlete. Muscular legs from playing indoor field hockey. A determined gait. She wore shorts, the tight ones, almost as if painted on her hips and ass. They were pale pink, and she'd smiled when she got a glimpse of herself in the small mirror in her room. She looked naked even with the shorts on. And she liked it and wanted that, the fabric holding her tight along her inner legs, like a hand. She wanted a hand.

As she passed a small farm, a gust of sea-borne wind blew through branches filled with flowers. She picked a red bloom that had fallen to the ground. And a few steps later, picked a handful of green grapes from a vine, oblivious to the rooster whose duty it was to announce the sun and protect lovers. The music percolated straight to her brain through the earpieces. She knew that she was supposed to be listening to the wind singing amidst the rocks and plants, and the waves, and the early birds, but that was not her, and she did not give into it. She had kept the earphones in even during the few times she had let the young son of her landlord come over and fuck her.

She reached the hotel before everyone else. She found no fresh underwear in her locker, so she stripped off the gym shorts and slipped the hotel's austere black maid's outfit over her nakedness. It was a practical dress buttoned in front with large translucent plastic buttons that traveled along a thin white strip from collar to hem. The laundry lady had tied the top eyelet with a red ribbon that specifically identified her. She kept her red lace brassiere on under the cotton outfit. It felt as if it was going to be a special day.

She took a mouthful of grapes again, resting in a small white ceramic bowl.

The hotel was lodged in a small valley facing a sheltered bay. The top floors offered a view well above the treetops. From there, the sea changed colors as the hours passed. She spent a lot of time looking at the sea. It was why she had kept this job. That, and the lovers.

She could not imagine a better place to remain isolated as the world demanded. Here, on this island, she could confine easily—she had the sun, the sea, and the occasional sex whenever she wanted it. Most of the time, she did not need to, but sometimes she just had to, especially when the pictures on the digital camera, kept on the lovers' bedside table, became too much for her to ignore.

She could not resist another grape. They were juicy and delicious and tasted exactly the same as the ones she had eaten earlier that morning. The laundry lady had left them there for the staff when she dropped off the clean dresses.

Her schedule that day would unfold as per routine. The manager, glad to have an efficient worker, let her decide the order of her day. She always kept the "lovers'" room for last.

More than once, she had entered the adjoining room in the early morning, pressed her ear on the locked door that led to their bedroom, and listened. Sometimes she heard them, witnessing by sound alone the surreal symphony of moans, words spoken, silences of voices, and the stinging sound of slaps on naked flesh.

She walked into their empty suite; as usual the rooms smelled lovely, especially then, with the tall white lilies with thick green stems standing gracefully in a transparent, equally tall vase. Their fragrance mixed with the undeniable scent of morning sex filling the bedroom.

She went straight to their bathroom, as she always did, and lifted the cap off his perfume. With his scent now on her, she went about tidying the room. Whatever clutter there was, she organized it, until she got to the terrace. Theirs was the only room in the hotel with such a terrace, and there, she found his jogging clothes. He always hung them on a chair to dry. She picked them up, and as always, she first brought his shirt to her face. Then she turned back inside where, enveloped in her own secrecy, she took in a deep breath of his still-wet shorts. For that moment, she was one with him. More intimate than lovers, she thought.

That day, she was done early. She picked up the camera that rested at its usual place on his bedside. She had the same one back home, a Sony 100 that captured every iota of light. It would take pictures even in darkness, even without a flash. His was the latest model, even in dim light it could capture flesh in the softest of tones.

She settled down on the carpet, facing the window to the terrace. Sunlight streamed through the fluttering linen curtains, caressing her naked inner thighs as she stretched her legs out to face the sky. She was pretty sure that they would not be back for a while, although strangely she did not care about that any longer. She almost wanted to be discovered and let it all unfold and shape the hours to come. Knees slightly bent, she parted her dress, leaving her seductive nakedness just a fingertip away. She flipped open the camera screen, made sure the light intensity was maximized, and scrolled through the recent photographs. There were many new ones. They were formidable. Her fingers started their dance, one hand on her and another on the screen. She scanned through the images quickly until she reached the video section. It was hidden in a side bar with others she had not seen yet.

She leans back and fully takes in the impact of the moving images. She moans as she sees Gabriella being tied up to the thick, metal hook, painted white and fixed high above the bed frame. Her wrists are bound up by one of the many cotton bandanas she herself folded and stored in the past.

The camera managed to pick up Gabriella's tan lines even in the dimmed luminance of the room. It picked up the red lines of pure pleasure she felt as he swung the thin, white rope over her buttocks. A phone charger? she guessed as she pulled hers out of her pocket and struck herself. Just to feel it. And it was surprising, and smooth, surprisingly smooth and powerful. It actually hurt. She tried again, and again. She looked at the screen and she saw how he stroked the girl several times with the rope but how only a few of them were really meant to hurt. He was gentle with her. She almost wanted him to hit her harder.

The thick green stem of the calla lilies dripped cool and firm between her legs. She became so intent on the screen, in her own pleasure, in the sun finding its way into her, that she did not hear the quiet key in the door or the light footsteps. She did not notice Gabriella watching her quietly for a little while, from the other room, and then tiptoe backward and close the door silently behind her.

She kept the camera intensity on high. It was her secret message to him. She left the room, eyes dreamy, almost in a daze of guilt and pleasure.

Her shift was done. She was already in the locker room, about to change, when the manager called her. "Mia," he said, please go speak to the client in Room 518. He's waiting for you at the cafe on the veranda."

Though her face did not show it, she immediately got worried. Was it about the camera, or something else? She needed it to be there already and so she hurried over.

He was seated alone at a far table, the one shaded by the large carob trees. Nervously, she came closer until she was standing right in front of him, hands by her side, noticing only now that, in her rush, she had missed the middle button of her dress, and surely he could see skin if he paid attention. She decided not to fix it. He looked at her, smiling. She relaxed a bit. He did not seem angry. He lifted his eyes, took off the sunglasses and with a nod, asked her to take a seat. "Do you know the legend of the Minotaur, Miss. . . ?"

"Mia. And yes on the Minotaur." Her eyes saw him, really, for the first time. She was at an age when everything seemed to be unfolding like a movie. He liked it that way. He did not rush her, and he took his time to look at her through pale blue eyes for a while longer, trying to read her mind, and let her read his. And then he asked her, "Would you have dinner with me tonight?"

His question took her by surprise. Moments before she thought she was going to be scolded for invasion of privacy, and now she was being asked to a private rendezvous.

She was surprised but not totally stunned. "Why tonight?"

"Because it's the full moon."

She pictured them together in the setting sun and she said, "Yes, gladly." She shifted her gaze slightly, a shy smile on her lips, "But why the Minotaur?"

He smiled back. "Because he gets activated at the full moon."

SHE REALIZED THAT SHE DIDN'T HAVE TIME to go back to her place and return in time for dinner. She needed some clothes, though.

She remembered the laundry lady. Mia knew that she lived somewhere close by. She remembered the grapes. Maybe she lived on the farm that she always walked past on her way to work. She put her earphones in and cranked the volume up as she ran to what turned out indeed to be where the laundress lived.

The older woman welcomed her and recognized the urgency in her eyes. She had been young once. She understood. She remembered the fervor of a full moon by the purple sea in the middle of summer, when the sap of trees flows out in thick resin. In those nights, the moon itself seems like a giant silver disc high above, about to release all the sperm of the sky —of Ouranos over Gaia—a fragment of a primordial time that reappeared every month, thousands and thousands of decades later. She had pressed a few more grapes into Mia's mouth, almost in a motherly fashion, encouraging her to go forth, fearless of age and taboos. She had lived well herself, and still did, and now almost felt as if she was reliving it all over again through the smile of this strange blonde, bouncing creature who had always been kind to her at the hotel.

She found her a precious garment she had kept for years, one left unclaimed at the hotel. It was silk, a light olive color, shimmering to an almost orange tone when it moved and caught the light. It draped itself deliciously over her naked body as if a foil destined for her. She kept on the red brassiere, not knowing why. Was she not destined to be devoured? That was clear to her. Maybe she kept it on because of her wish to impress the older woman, to show her that she was a proper girl. She was ready to leave when the woman threw a dark pink scarf around her shoulders and, in so doing, brought her closer and gave her a good luck kiss on her forehead.

Man

HE OWNED THE SOUNDS OUT THERE on the far side of the island. All of them had to have a meaning, for he was alone, and the only one to want to hear them. There was no one else to delegate the shared burden to of finding the origins of each sound: the dove's love calls, the waves crashing far below to his right as he ran back home, the wind whistling through the needles of pine trees high above. All primitive reverberations that echoed through time and surrounded him and only him.

He stopped under the shade of a tall tree in a small glade of pines. The sun had just risen, but as it is familiar on those isles, it climbed into the sky at full speed, and the tree offered protection. He spotted a couple of doves. They were gray as pearls and seemed gentle in every move they made. He cupped his hands together, left over right, and with both thumbs parallel brought them to his open lips. He blew softly into the cavity of his linked hands and mimicked their sound. They responded, and they spoke back and forth for a little while. Then he smiled at the thought of how similar his cupped hands were now to the mystical openness of a woman. He would play music to his wife soon, after she had her fill of sleep. There was no point trying earlier; he had learned that long ago. So instead, he ran early. He saw the sunrises. He talked in his mind to birds. He went for a dip in the clear, cool morning water and then finally went back to her.

"Doubly salted," she moaned in her early-morning wakefulness as she let her tongue lick his skin. He saw her body unfold as she reached for him. The white sheets curling away from her nakedness, like a receding wave of fabric, exposing her luscious curves when he parted her legs, her inner folds. His fingers went to his mouth. Saliva poured out, as it always did whenever he got aroused, a thin stream that he applied on her, finding her pleasure in slow movements, his middle finger repeatedly moving over the exposed crux, her mouth busy on him now as he lay by her side, and as she swung her thigh over his face for a long moment of playing time. Everything was always foreplay, and they both worked at it. He slapped her and, even though her mouth was full, heard a moan. He slapped her fragile nakedness. The slap was just hard enough for her to feel the exquisite pain and yet not injure her. He needed her pussy.

In the morning light her flesh looked beautiful, streaked by the glow of his saliva on the untanned area. Always, she wanted to go completely nude on the beach, but always he forbade it.

Earlier in the morning, as he whistled to the doves under the tree, he had seen the maid walk along the path on the other side of the beach and the hotel. For a moment, he'd really thought she was naked under the black sweater. It was an idyllic sight, and as long as he believed it, that illusion became his personal reality. He was astonished and excited, like a kid in a candy store. A half-naked woman, the intimate half walking fast and serenely towards him as a mythological presence on a predetermined task. He could feel the weight of her breast under the black knit sweater. They moved in unison with his own heartbeat. Only much later did he see the red lace brassiere that held them back.

THEY HAD UPGRADED THE WI-FI at the hotel and he could work from here. He ran some of the family's holdings. It could have been a tedious job, but he had grown into it and now was making decisions that shaped the future of the company. His father relied on him more and more. Meanwhile, when not working he ran, swam, ate, and fucked, all the while together with his wife, the woman he loved.

"Where are we eating tonight?" he asked her.

There were only a few choices. Either the hotel restaurant facing the beach, or further back on the hill, at a place where the cook prepared goat meat just the way she liked, cooked in a sweet fresh tomato sauce, with green beans from the garden on the side. There they would drink the local white wine—

crisp, fresh, almost translucent—that shone bright in the late evening sun. They drank it like water in short glasses with a simple grooved line two-thirds up. The owner always over-filled their glasses in an act of zealous excitement whenever they went there. He was charmed by them for, whenever they were together in public, they exuded the magic of happiness that people immediately recognize—not an ostentatious display of affection but the small nuances that made a couple solid, gesture by gesture. Sometimes, at dessert time, the owner brought out the even smaller glasses into which he poured the sweet wine that he made himself from the grapes grown in the nearby field. She loved it. This was turbid, and it felt exactly as if she was drinking a love potion.

She told him, "It makes me feel so special to drink it here in the valley, where it was made, served by the hands that made it. Like an elixir of sorts."

And she would drink it with her eyes closed, wishing wonders as the sweetness swept through her—and she fully aware of how lucky she was just then, in that moment, there with him to share it with.

From the small terraces of that tavern, the moon could be seen rising out of the sea. Tonight was to be a full moon. It would be nice to go there and see it rise.

The only other choice for dinner was to take the small boat from the hotel and coast around the bay up to a small dock where they moored. There, he would help her off the boat in a gallant fashion, knowing full well that she could easily leap unto the wooden platform, but knowing also that she liked the outstretched helping hand. And the fact that he kept her hand in his as they walked to what they called their "fish place." There you had to call ahead, because they did not always have a fresh catch. But when they did, you actually felt as if you were eating the sea itself. It was the simplest of food. Almost elemental. Unaffected by pretense or attempts at embellishing the white flesh of the fish except for the side sauce made with olive oil and lemon juice, adding a touch of the fragrant earth. When they had finished eating, he would steer her boat back home to the hotel, and she would stand up straight, legs apart, at the front of the boat, holding onto the taut nautical rope. He would keep his loving eyes on her, observing her slender shape becoming less and less visible in the waning light.

"Let's try the fish place?" he asked again inquisitively.

It was a loaded question. He knew very well that that night she would disappear again as she did every year on the full August moon. She would leave him just before sunset, only to reappear just after sunrise. Always that night. Always the same place. He had somehow reluctantly agreed to it several years before as a prerequisite to their relationship.

She looked up at him with the softest of smiles. "You know you'll eat without me tonight, my love," and said, and went back to painting her toenails a crimson red. She always did that, too.

The whole ritual was becoming more and more vexing and obscene to him as years went by. He was not sure how long he could let it happen with so much secrecy involved. In despair, he reached out for a cotton tip, and in the gentlest way possible, let it tickle his ear. He needed the caress, the small pleasure, just then. He looked away. The mysterious night schedule baffled him, yet he was too proud to ask any more questions. He never had and was resolute that he never would.

He caught his reflection in the old bathroom mirror. He gazed at his own eyes. For years he had forbidden himself to look at his own gaze, but now he did. He let his eyes lose themselves, and in that private moment, decided that he would not dine alone that night.

HE HAD REALIZED THAT SOMEONE WAS LOOKING at his camera and the pictures. He knew it because he did not personally like the full brightness of the screen and yet the camera often seemed to revert itself to that intensity setting. It was not a factory feature; he had checked. So it must be the maid! Instead of being upset about it, he played with it. He and Gabriella rarely looked at the images together once they were taken. At any rate, Gabriella did not like to see herself or, even less, hear herself. And he didn't need to look at pictures at all. He had her in real life.

No, the intent of taking the picture was taking the pictures.

That was it. It excited him in its pure essence—recording an act that seemed to defeat all representation, and yet had been represented at all times and ages—from the initial flanks on pottery of ancient civilizations, and then from pottery to sculptures, and frescoes to paintings, all marvelously displayed in academic museums all over the world, corrupting the innocent visitor with their magical and often not-so-hidden language. He was merely duplicating the artists of previous millennia with today's technology. But now he knew (or somehow felt at least) that through his photos he might have a possible visitor, his own private visitor for his own private exhibition. He liked that. He filmed for her now. Sometimes he even fucked for her.

Having sex was a form of communication, a way to symbolize in the flesh the seamless harmony he felt with Gabriella. And having a lot of sex, making love several times a day, was something altogether different. It became a language of its own. There were no blank pages, no heavy punctuation. It was, in essence, a scent, an atmosphere that they breathed in together. There was none of the awkwardness of having to rediscover the other, because the other was never far. He and she inhaled each other in large vats of oxygen, like high-flying birds in the ozone layer, like swimmers within each other's stroke, the air and the water becoming one in the constant forward motion, physical encounters and the flow of the days moving in unison.

He lusted for her at all times. He wanted her always and always showed it. At times she was just too tired to even think of it, so he would let her sleep. And later in her sleep, in the middle of the night, he would find her and ever so slowly find his way into her. And into her sleep. To be closer to her. Closer to her sleeping soul. A step away from death.

She would moan a bit and let him move a bit. He knew that it would most likely lead to nothing but a deep, passionate hug, but he did it anyway. He did it because, though he did not admit it, he did love the hug. Loved meeting like pieces of a puzzle, finding each other in anonymous darkness. And also because, at times, this deepest of night penetration led to something else, something usually a lot dirtier and more involved than bright daytime sex would ever allow. As if, in the deep hours of the night, darkness was unveiled, and bodies and minds allowed to drift further. That was when she talked the most, revealing and melting away in her own words, saying out loud unthinkable hidden thoughts. That is when words took on another meaning, when they became oil and allowed a clear passage into another world. They both knew what to tell each other. He was the one who had started it, telling her within the first encounters about his fantasies and urges. Now, on this prolonged beach hotel exile, he had to be everything--stranger and husband. The two welded together as he tied her up to the hook and abused her, only to release her arms later and let her tightly embrace the width of his broad shoulders.

He knew how she liked it, deep and hard, sometimes slow and other times so fast, with the glass dildo deep in her ass.

BUT FOR ALL OF THAT, HE STILL DIDN'T KNOW where she was going, as she did every year on the very full moon. He knew better than to ask. For one thing, it would go against everything he whispered to her at night. For another, he could feel that she begged him without words not to.

As much as some of their words became actions, many small acts took on the power of words: the Ella Fitzgerald and the *Goldberg Variations* she chose to play on the hotel's only gramophone, made available to their suite alone, while getting ready. The smile she kept on her lips as she hummed along to the melodies from an era much older than their usual Radiohead. The way she looked away from him as she painted her nails the vividness of wine. All silent yet clear.

He had spoken to Mia earlier and she had agreed to meet him for dinner, and that knowledge alone would make it a little easier for him to watch the crimson toes walk out the door.

He was not jealous. He knew that was a self-destructive emotion. He also did not want to be alone during the magical night. He had been in previous years, but not in this one. There was just so much chess he could play by himself against the computer, not knowing what his love, his wife, was doing—yet knowing that, somehow, she was breathing the same air as he was. He wanted so much to think that every-

thing about this succession of events breathed enchantment—
as if the night existed in essence only, as if it had happened already, a moment in time carved out high up in a rock. As if it
was a line he could see but not run his finger against, immu-
table and decadent.

He had met her by enchantment as well. One day she
had appeared on a bike in Central Park as he himself was
coasting after having raced several loops. He followed her and
spoke to her and almost bit his own head off later on when he
realized that he had forgotten to ask for her phone number.
He'd come back the next day at the same time, and the following one, but she was nowhere to be seen. He had waited for
her on a bench, looking for her shape to fly by in vain.

And then a week later he had walked right into her at a deserted Soho streetcorner, late one afternoon, when he had no
business being there. Her face had been half-hidden by a scarf
against the cold. He had at first seen only the lower half beneath
the helmet and glasses while on the bike, and then her eyes and
gentle forehead. In his mind, though, he'd had no trouble rec-
reating her, and this time around he had asked her to stay with
him and have dinner that same evening. He was not going to
lose her again. That was over three years ago. Now he was
about to have another dinner, with another woman.

He had decided to shave off the beard he'd grown over the
last two weeks, partly to become fresh anew and partly to re-

spond in similar fashion to the toenail polish. Although he wasn't jealous, he wasn't particularly pleased either. He used the three-blade razor a good friend had recently given him. With each added blade to the razor, he could measure his age in the world. He had started with one lousy blade as a teenager. He was hoping to make it to six.

He used the shaving cream they had bought together in a specialty store in London. That too was like magic. The smallest amount of product created a thick, luscious foam over his face and neck. With each stroke of the blade, he repainted his face and its contours. He watched himself shave meticulously, almost as a spectator sport.

Halfway through, he remembered to honor his dead relatives, one name for each stroke, one remembrance and utterance for each name, so they might live a little longer, even if it was only in a span of his gradually reappearing features. Finally, he smiled in the mirror as he prayed solemnly to all of them—his dead ones. He prayed this way every time, but only for the departed. He knew he had no control over the living. He felt ready.

He wanted to be out of the door before Gabriella was.

Wife

SHE KNEW IT WAS SUNRISE OUTSIDE. She knew it even in the depth of her sleep. Her body told her. And the absence of his breath and weight next to her told her as well. She knew it and she did not care. Not at all. She wanted the full eight hours.

Eventually, she heard him come back to the room, leave his shoes at the door, and walk quietly to her side of their bed. He looked at her, shirt in hand. And almost instinctively, she raised her hand and felt his manhood through the thin fabric of his running shorts. The shorts were still wet from his run and swim, and with eyes still lazy with sleep, she found him. Through the opening of his shorts, she brought him to her mouth. "Doubly salted," she said, and smiled at him. She did it with the desire to breathe him in—to take in his scent at the same time as she let him fill her mouth and got ready for him to grow in it.

She had been lingering in bed, waiting for him in her sleep. Her thin, tanned body stretched playfully along the night sheets where dry oval spots were the barely visible vestiges of last night's play. She had shaved everything yesterday. "Double nakedness," he answered as he leaned further over and found her in turn.

During the night he had confessed to her that he would always let the mosquitoes bite him whenever they landed on him rather than have them feed on her. She loved him for that, and she loved him more every time he took her. The carnal presence when he penetrated her, the taste of his lips, the scent of his skin, all becoming hers—orchestrating her own private sunrise. And each time, she opened her soul wider and let the wave of his love sweep her over and over, and she loved him back in return. And she told him so. "I love you, "she whispered in the middle of the night, with the purest of intent, as he ever-so-gently pushed himself into her again. She felt the fullness of his girth and she settled on it, and they both went back to sleep, content in the certainty of previous and future fucks.

At times, when things got heated, when he let his mind take over, he would reach for the camera. At first, she had been surprised and shy, but over time, she had started to enjoy the lens like eyes, and the screen like a third person. Gradually, she ended up doing things for him on camera that she never thought she would do, and he filmed her with the love of the moment, not even thinking about looking at it again. It was almost a philosophical vision of things, a way of documenting their privacy, a way to cheat death somehow. As if recording the act itself was defying nature and passion, a private moment of life stolen away on a digital screen, sucked into a vortex of virtual clouds, against all primal expectations.

At the present time, after the morning run, there was no one watching. No cameras locked on them as she felt his fingers slip into her.

One finger. Then two.

She moaned. Her body arched in pleasure and defiance.

In the near distance, the sun hit the surface of the sea and the breeze picked up some more, infiltrating the room with warmth and murmurs. Soon she was done. She could not last a second longer with his face on her. She pushed his head away laughingly, her body trembling. Only the flowing breeze could touch her now. Anything else would be too much.

He knew it.

He came back around and laced himself against her frame. She tilted her head sideways. They kissed and tasted each other and themselves.

Aries had been caught in the same act when, unaware that the sun was up, he still had his own face buried in Aphrodite while the other Pantheon gods watched, laughing from high above. They say he created the rooster that day from the body of his sentinel friend who fell asleep during his watch.

Somewhere close by, the island's roosters were singing their songs, and they could hear them from their own bed.

Later, she made coffee for him in a small, thin, ceramic cup. It was an added luxury from the hotel, and she knew it was a special attention to her from the hotel owner.

SHE HAD BEEN GOING THERE ever since she was a teenager—first with her parents, then in the company of a lover or two, and now for several years with her husband.

The owner's business had kept expanding. In the ensuing years he had bought many more properties, and he rarely came back to this one. Yet he always came by when Gabriella was there.

He was arriving that day. He didn't even really need to tell her. At night she would see him, as she did every year on the full August moon.

As usual, with time, all her clothes had become stiff in the salty island air and the daily sun. She was well aware of this, which was why she had kept one dress protected in her luggage. She always brought the same one, or a similar version of it. She was going to wear it that night.

It had started when she was seventeen. Her parents had brought her and her brother for the same two weeks every year. Back then, the place had just been bought by an enterprising young man in his thirties who seemed to be everywhere at once. He worked at the desk, the restaurant, sometimes even the kitchen. A native of the island, he was the one to recommend day trips and give advice on anything island-related. He was the son of farmers, and throughout his youth, his body had been shaped according to the constraints of his life in the fields and the hikes in the hills with the herd of goats. His form following his function, his neck became strong, his shoulders wide. He had big hands with long fingers. She loved his hands even before she knew why. His blue eyes were deeply seated in his tanned face, almost like an anomaly on that island, like a vestige from invaders long ago. He was handsome.

Also, he had the kindest of smiles.

Over the years, he had watched Gabriella grow and unfold in front of his summer eyes, and as years went by, she, in turn, learned to see him differently with each passing season. By the time she reached sixteen, she realized that she had fallen in love with him. At seventeen, she was ready to give him her virginity. She knew he would want it. The year before, they had kissed, and when she reached for him, he had said, "Next year, my dove."

During that year, she had blossomed into a full woman. Her breasts filled all her bras perfectly. Her mouth became ripe. Her hips began to move in tandem with her inner desires. She had had an active year. She had taken boyfriends on whom she practiced for the two weeks of August. She had let them do everything to her—every single thing except to take her and take over her womanhood, for that was reserved to her love, her white bull who waited for her on the island.

The minotaur was born from the fateful coalescence of a queen and a white bull. Dedalus created the instrument of seduction, a hollow bovine shape into which she strategically positioned herself, before he had to create the labyrinth to hide the final product of that union.

At first, he had said "no" again. He was too old for her, he said. She should keep it for someone more suitable, more in line with her faith, her family, and her future life. He told her that he was about to leave the island and study real hotel management. He was going to open another hotel elsewhere and would have no time for her. He told her there was no to-morrow for them.

"That is exactly why we have to do it today," she had replied.

He'd been stunned. She was so young and here she was looking up at him with full lips on a mouth that promised sun and squashed strawberries. With those wanting lips she told him that all the signs had aligned—that the rare cactus flower had blossomed that morning, and that tonight, Saturn, Jupiter, and a full moon, would line up and shine for them only. She told him it was destiny.

She had told her parents that she was having a sleepover at her friend's further inland. Once out of sight, she walked straight to the hut he had directed her to go to. It was white throughout, both outside and inside walls covered in the same pure washed paint that locals applied every other year over old stones and mortar. She was ready for him, inside and outside, like she had never felt before.

The cabin was part of a small winery, and he helped her up onto the makeshift bed he had contrived for them on thick wooden planks that covered a large vat into which, each fall, the grapes were pressed by dancing feet. There, he had taken her. And as he did, she had screamed to her heart's content, staining the wood already red from past pressed wines.

He came back every year, officially to check on the property for ten days or so, but ultimately to be there when the full August moon filled up the white cabin with silver light. Right after their first encounter, he had bought that land with its simple house. He continued to make wine there every fall and then drank it at every full moon throughout the year, waiting for the one night when he was coerced by oath to return to her in their cabin.

For the last several years, he had not even shown up at the hotel itself. His family had grown, and his business had grown as well. Nowadays, he flew in by helicopter to the other side of the island, and he waited for her in the cabin, year after year. And she too returned for that one night, every year, her dress a variant of the one she wore for him on the very first night—her eyes pure, her toenails crimson, just as they were when she was seventeen.

The day before, she had known that her husband was filming when he tied her up, blindfolded, and whispered in her ear over the music. She knew he was recording as he slapped her and whipped her with the wide leather belt she had given him. She remembered when she bought the belt from the Hermes store, knowing that one day it would perhaps resonate loudly against her naked skin. She remembered smiling while the felt its weight in her hands and seeing the Asian salesgirl smile back at her. Had that been a smile of sheer politeness, or had the salesgirl known what she was thinking? She'd seemed Japanese and bondage maybe not so foreign to her, as she had witnessed in his Japanese photography book collection. Bondage had been intriguing at first but then became fabulously enticing once she had tasted it. She did not see it as relinquishing control. To her, it was a dance. And he was her favorite partner.

Earlier in the day, stumbling onto the partially disrobed maid, her black dress hanging loosely over her shoulders, her eyes riveted on the sea, sky, and light, Gabriella had thought at once, *What a magical sight!* not the least judgmental, and had remained silent. She hadn't wanted to disturb her—not then, when everything had to go smoothly before her evening escapade. Looking secretly at the maid and absorbing the full impact of it, she also thought, *My husband would love to take a picture of this.* She could imagine the lovely, almost nude profile of the girl on the screen, framed by the white blooms of the calla lilies that always arrived the day before the full moon, the maid's short blonde hair a perfect echo to the bright sunlit petals.

Gabriella had remained at the door, watching just a little longer, fascinated and even slightly aroused. Over time, the maid had slowly become part of their spoken and unspoken fantasies on this trip. In her own mind, she had enjoyed the idea of sleeping with her and in words, at night, alone with him, she had even pretended to do it for him.

She had stepped back ever so silently then and left without a sound.

MUCH LATER IN THE DAY, SHE WAS ALMOST ready to leave the hotel room for her rendezvous when her husband entered, shaved and anointed. She smiled almost imperceptibly. He captured that instant and smiled back. She knew she was in no position to ask him what his plans were. Instead, she turned around and asked for help to fasten the last few buttons of her dress. It took a little while. They were fragile buttons made of the same fabric as the dress itself. His hands were shaking a bit. He was wondering if someone else would duplicate this task later in the night.

Finally, he was done. He took a long, deep look at her honey-brown eyes before turning around and leaving the room. She looked at the door as it closed behind him. He had blown a kiss from afar and she so wanted to feel its full impact. Yet it felt somehow hollow and left her somewhat empty.

She knew that what she was doing was tough on him. It was becoming tough on her too, she reflected. At night, they sometimes freely spoke about all the things that they had or could have done with other men and women. The cocks licked, the asses pressed open, the flesh bruising itself against each other. They traced the shape of things that could happen and those that would happen.

This was different, though. It lived intensely in the power of its own silence, her chosen lack of words, a secret no one could probe and that she was not ready to share, though she allowed her body to do so.

She put on the earphones. She really needed the headspace that only that kind of music could give her, letting her forget herself in a cloud of sonic vibrations. As she logged in, there was only one other listener on the whole island: Pinkpussy18. She smiled. What a funny and unusual name, she thought as she gathered the last details before leaving. She closed the door and made it to the waiting boat on the side of the hotel pier. In the distance she thought she could make out the maid moving on the path towards the hotel.

NIGHT
Maid

HE HAD TOLD HER WHERE TO MEET HIM. She knew the small stretch of beach well. It was a hidden cove away from the crowd. Sometimes during her lunchbreak, she would either swim there or walk between the rocks and sunbathe in the anonymous glare of the summer. She knew that perhaps, at times, she was being watched. It did not bother her. She would put the earphones in and forget the nakedness. She never stayed long enough for anyone to approach her, at any rate. She just wanted the kiss of the sun all over her exposed body, a world away from her distant home country.

She had seen him swim in the past from the terrace of their suite. So it was not a total surprise, when she reached their rendezvous, to see him at the edge of the water, mimicking the backstroke as if grabbing at unseen thoughts and angels and invisible flowers. She watched him for a little while, privately.

Earlier, she had also seen the boat leave, a scratch in the sea.

She had used the old woman's mascara. It was almost all dried up in its little plastic box from an era long gone, but it did the trick. For perfume she had squeezed flowers on her dry hands and rubbed them on her neck and shoulders. A thin belt separated her lovely shape in two—pure and impure.

He turned around. His shirt was open. She could see the hair on his chest. Even in the waning light, a few were gray amid the blonde. She liked that and smiled as she saw him try to tuck the shirt in as fast as possible. She left her sandals behind and ambled barefoot towards him. As she got closer, she was reminded of how much taller he was. She tiptoed to him, looked him in the eyes and silently untucked his shirt, unbuttoned the thick, dark blue discs, and released his chest once again.

"It's better like this," she said. "You should be comfortable."

It was not an overtly erotic gesture, so he let it happen without reaching for her. He seemed to feel the heat, though, and enjoy it, too.

They drank the wine. In her own glass she saw the reflection of the nascent moonlight, and drank its glow, the cup becoming a divine chalice in her hand. She looked at him with a gleam in her eye, thinking how both of them, separated only by the thinnest of layers, were waiting to satisfy the souls whose invisible weight was filling the evening air.

She said nothing, just got closer to him and could smell the perfume she stole every day from his bathroom spray. She was at ease. She knew him, better than he thought she did.

She lit all the candles he had brought while he got the table ready. They were both moving in unison and silence, as if everything that needed to be said already had, and been sealed.

She loved sitting at the table he had set for them, her feet caressing the water as the occasional wave came high enough up the beach. And she shivered with anticipation when she felt his fingers linger on the back of her neck with the softest of touch. The surface of the silver sea rustled at the same instant under a sudden gust of breeze.

The food was all she wanted just then. He had arranged for salads and somehow still warm *rougets*, caught that day and fried in the lightest of batter. He showed her how to eat them.

"The skin and fins taste like chips, believe me," he said as she initially seemed reluctant to eat the translucent tail.

It did taste good, but she left the other tails for him. Everything tasted good at the end, and they swallowed it with sips of wine and started laughing at the beauty of it. He washed his hands in the seawater right by the feet of the table. She did the same and, for an instant, the saltiness of his finger slipped along her lips.

"So you saw the pictures?" he asked, eyebrows reaching towards the bridge of his strong nose. An inquiring smile on his face illuminated the question.

"Yes," she admitted without losing his gaze. Then there was another silence. They were so close to each other across the small table, the river of moonlight in the water destined to make landfall at their feet. His hand caressed the side of her face, her hair, the back of her ear.

"So which picture did you like best?" he murmured.

It was a silly question, he realized as soon as he said it. Words were moving faster than his sense of style and timing. He winced a little as he heard himself say it.

"The ones of the Perriand Bibliotheque," she said without missing a beat. He was floored: Everything about the answer was perfect. She had diverted his insolence by ignoring it and revealed a keen sense of observation and knowledge. Few people knew of Charlotte Perriand, the superlative female mid-century designer, and fewer still would have been able to appreciate the piece of furniture he had built a whole room around. A beautiful object, a beautiful moment. From that object a rainbow of other beautiful moments would flow. That was the power of such good design. And she recognized it! He looked at her with a slight air of reverence.

"It's so marvelous," he said, meaning her answer.

"Yes, it's a unique piece. I never saw one like that before."

They talked furniture. It was secret language known to a privileged few who did the homework.

The wine settled in. It traveled down her veins. It flowed into the confines of her brain. Quite naturally, without really thinking about it, she reached into her dress and removed the bra. It was getting tight, and maybe she just wanted him to guess the shape of her curves.

She straightened up. He took the bra in his hand and, in slow motion, brought it to his face, inhaling her scent while focusing his gaze, through the thin fabric, on the marvelous outline of her raised nipples, determined not to miss any memory of her.

Both sensations took her breath away. He was silent, his eyes like lenses, and she projected herself onto him. She wanted to. She felt it was her duty. She wanted to fill the screen of his being. Earlier, she had guessed his nakedness under the white cotton slacks when he kneeled to open the first bottle of wine, and she had enjoyed it. And now she enjoyed exposing herself as good as naked in front of him.

She was completely and utterly naked a little later in the bedroom.

He had gone for a moment into the bathroom, and in that same moment she had slipped off the dress. It now lay on the wooden chair along, with her scarf and belt. She sat at the edge of the bed, elbows on her knees, sipping from the short glass. He walked in, looked at her, and uncovered her nakedness.

She looked straight back at him, and he saw her nod, pointing to the hook above the bed.

He went to the terrace windows, pulled the white linen curtains open, and let the silver light dilute itself all over her tied-up body. In a flash, he thought he saw a nocturnal bird fly across the face of the moon.

"I want to be with you," he whispered as he turned back and looked at her. She could see the leather belt in his hands, exactly as she had intended, waiting for the first lash to strike her. By then, the room had turned a darker shade, almost like the glow of the red wine in the glass by the candle. She watched it for a moment longer, just before he blindfolded her with the same cotton bandana she had seen him use in the videos. And then the slaps came, slow and deliberate. She felt the exquisite pain almost as if it was outside her body.

He came by her, and his mouth touched her lips. She opened her mouth, and he let the icy wine go from his lips to hers. He let it run along the seared skin of her ass. He asked her ever so tenderly how was she doing. Did she want more?

"Yes," she said. "Yes, please."

Instead, he strapped her neck. She was on her knees. She felt herself drifting away. "Stay," he told her. "Stay with me.".

And she did. She let go, and when he did too, life rushed back to her brain, and she felt him hard and deep and driving fast into her—splitting her in half. She could hear him so clearly as well. Every sensation amplified, she begged for more. She wanted that again. She had never felt anything like it. The bondage released her into another sphere. She was riding the light of countless moons and unsung winds as he took full possession of her, of her pussy, of her ass, of her being. She saw red—and she stayed there between sleep and devotion until the very first sign of daylight. Before the roosters even perceived it, and without a sound, she retrieved the dress, the scarf, her belt, and the sandals. She was gone before he even realized it. She ran back home barefoot in her tight pink shorts, like an animal free in the cool morning air.

Man

He had made plans for dinner. He was good at making plans. Gabriella was not. When he got upset about that, she said, "Imagine how terrible it would be if we both made plans, darling." She was right. Instead, he became more adapt at arranging everything and making the daily routine seamless so that they could float on it, and she could be queen.

He played chess, and Gabriella played checkers, one move at a time, and she won. He'd learned how to play the chess game of daily life. No room for second guesses, the big picture condensed in pixels.

He had told Mia to meet him in the little creek that stood on the other side of their hotel beach, away from everyone. He had arranged for the table and the food. The bottles of white wine were to be left floating in a mesh bag secured between some rocks. He had arranged for candle lanterns as well, just three or four of them around the confines of the narrow strip of sand.

He'd checked it all out.

In the distance, he'd heard Gabriella's boat leave. She could not see him in his hidden enclave. He could imagine her sitting for once at the helm of the ship, the thick polished wooden bar in her right hand as she maneuvered around the two rocks at the outlet of the bay. He knew she would bear left, and indeed, soon after, the echoing noise of the engine vanished out west. It almost felt liberating. The candles were still unlit. His night was to begin.

He'd looked at the water, the sun set behind the hotel. Yet somehow, a narrow ray of light had managed to find its way along the crest of the small lapping waves. A good omen, he'd been thinking. He relinquished these small signs in everyday life that became his personal symbols of fate and told him that everything was moving well.

He stood looking for a while at the sea, out west, where the water surface was still shining clear. Instinctively, in his mind, he saw himself swimming backstrokes. He could see the span of water that stood still ahead of him. Or behind him, he thought, smiling, the water ahead a heavy slice of colored sea. Its color would shift depending on how the sun penetrated it, either straight on or in a tangential arc. He moved his arms backward, imagining his fingers entering the mass of color with their own arc, mixing the deep blues, the light greens, the liquid emeralds with the white foam of his own motion. It was a silent explosion with each breath, witnessed only by the swimmer, and only if he rendered himself vulnerable enough to expose his flanks to the sky and allow his head to go down underwater with each stroke. It felt strangely akin to how he felt now, waiting for Mia to arrive. He was living all of this, his feet in the sand by the water's edge, his arms swinging like windmills in his dark blue, now unbuttoned cotton shirt.

He quickly buttoned it back up when he caught a glimpse of her, clumsily closing and tucking it while taking in her beauty. She looked royal in her simple elegance, her outfit the color of sunsets, a splinter of the horizon, an echo of the evening sky, her short hair uncombed and wild.

She pulsed forward and, before he knew it, unbuttoned his shirt again. It was surprisingly natural, as if she belonged to that beach and they belonged to that moment. "You have to be comfortable," she told him. And he was. There was something soothing in her voice, her demeanor. The air around them was warm, like a secluded embrace from land and sea all at once.

He took out the first of the wine bottles and uncorked it with a foldable corkscrew he had in his pants pocket. It was the only object in the light cotton pants. He pulled the cork out with the bottle between his legs, as his dad had taught him years before. The sound exploded around the alcove. A late bird flew away. They were utterly alone now.

"*L'Chaim!*" he said.

"*Prost!*"

They both drank from the short-stemmed glasses. He finished his in a long, slow, single twist of his wrist, almost as if to throw a gauntlet to fate. She sipped hers slowly, the rim of the glass suspended between the lips she had bitten red just before she walked onto the beach.

The table was sitting level right at the edge of the water. He had made sure of that. And now he placed the two wooden chairs, a faded blue, face to face, holding her seat as she settled down. He moved to the other side, his fingers tracing the back of her neck and shoulders as he passed behind her.

The salads were tossed from vegetables and fruit grown in the local farms right behind them—the goat cheese, the olives, even the flatbread. All had been produced in that isolated valley, fed by a delicate stream of fresh water. Even the wine came from a small winery further west along the coast, a short boat ride away.

He checked the time almost mechanically, as if it made a difference—the boat never came back till dawn.

"Nice vintage Submariner," she said, referring to his Rolex.

"You know your watches!" he said with a smile.

"Yes, I have always liked men's watches on women. One

day I'll get one."

"Are you hungry, dear Mia?"

"Yes, I'm starving," she lied.

She was mainly nervous and excited, but saying she was hungry was a good way to buy time. He knew that, and he smiled as he served the food, knowing that she would hardly touch it. He watched her with the adoration of an artist facing a new great work of art. Smiling at her as he talked to her, and then silent as he saw her reach to the inside of her dress and re-move, like the spine of one of their fish, the red lace brassiere he had caught a glimpse of, the taut fabric of the dress molding itself around her almost exposed nipples. He took the bra she handed him and eventually slipped it in his right pocket, next to the corkscrew.

Even before they were done drinking the wine and eating all the fish, he took her hand, and they left everything else be-hind. Someone was coming to clear it all up by early morning, before the sun rose.

She carried her sandals in her left hand, and they walked by the light of the moon. They both knew that they would walk back into the hotel through the rear-facing service en-trance. They both knew much and yet so little of each other.

She stopped him at the crest of the path, her face bathed by the moonlight.

"Whatever happens," she said, "remember that your pleas-ure is my pleasure. Do with me as you please."

"Oh, my Lord," he answered. "You are incredible! You are beautiful, and incredible." He felt his manhood against the metallic tool in his pocket, the heat of the night finding its way to the edge of his frame. "Your battle is my battle," he told her.

It was her turn to be stunned. "Why do you say that?" she whispered.

"I'm not sure. The words just appeared in my mind. Why do you ask?"

"I think you will soon find out."

They walked on, fingers interlocked, the pace faster as they got closer to the hotel.

THE SUGAR IN THE INTOXICATING SWEET WINE WAS their dessert, validating the hunger they felt rising for each other. It fueled his arm as he let the leather belt sting her buttocks, striking them with wide, red blemishes. Her bra held her wrists high up on the hook. Her remarkable body stood still even after several resounding slaps. She answered "Yes, please," when he asked her if she wanted more, but he knew that more would spoil the night. So he spun the belt around her neck instead, and as he pulled, he spread her open. His hand found her wet, and he took her without another thought. He counted to ten, released the strap, and moved even faster into her. Blood rushing back to her brain, she exploded towards him with her hips. That was when he saw

the small, scripted tattoo on her left flank. It read, *Your bat-*
tle is my battle.

He took her to sea, like a ship surfing effortlessly on wave
after wave of pleasure. He steered her until she pushed him
back and sat on him, her hands wide apart on his chest. He
swam deeper into her, and his hips lifted her as she stood
further up, resting on him only. His hands pressing hard on
her tender nipples as she came on the biggest of waves.

The sea itself had parted open, like an ancient Greek omen.

They'd slept, met again, soft and tender this time, and slept
again, and then she had been gone, before dawn. He had
opened the curtains to a dark sea. In the distance, he could
hear the engine of the boat returning. He'd showered and
dressed and waited on the terrace, his eyes fixed at the growing
outline of the morning earth.

He had left a large book of reproductions of paintings open
at the image of Botticelli's Venus.

> *Aphrodite is born again.*
> *Love arising from the sea.*
> *The foam on the waves originating from*
> *the father of Zeus, Kronos, the emasculated*
> *Titan from whose phallus the sperm came in*
> *contact with the fertile sea.*

His wife would see it.

Wife

THE WOODEN TILLER FELT HEAVY and meaningful in her hands. All she had to do was push or pull a little and the entire boat would shift course. Few tools have that intrinsic power— the capacity to determine destiny. Few tools except, perhaps, the human cock; she laughed at herself.

She was listening to the most amazing beat with her earphones. She and that other person—man or woman—Pink-Pussy18.

He was waiting for her on a narrow pier of wooden planks tied together over the water. The sea was alive with illuminated phosphorescent plankton, "phosies" she called them, and she could see his tall profile, a shade darker than the coming dawn, becoming clearer and clearer as she got closer. He tied the boat up for her, and she let herself slide straight into his arms. They lingered, alone in the deserted cove, away from life, as if floating over the deep moving water. And then, when they slowly walked back to solid land, he saw her beautiful dress flow sideways in a sudden gust of breeze as she preceded him up along the path to their annual meeting house. There, the white candles he had brought with him from the mainland were already lit. They met in silence. The sound of the cork, exploding out of the bottle he held between his knees, resonating even longer than she could remember. They drank the wine. They spoke little. There was much not to talk about.

Meeting there, in that way, was more like lifting an old instrument you loved, and playing from it the sweet sound of the music of your own soul. For some it was a game, but for them it meant that something had not yet died. They fed on each other, like lovers do, and the music became that much more beautiful. One note of ecstasy and tenderness at a time bounced forward and found another until they linked to each other and composed, under the silver light in the white room with the red stains, the harmony of a parallel life.

He sat down on a beautiful old chair, and she kneeled down on the fur, her face finding him as strong and virile as ever. She was gentle, though, and she was the one who sat on him, on the edge of the chair. His manhood filling her, his hands finding her, here and there. And later in defiance, and with the strength of an old bull, he stood up and took her to the stained wooden planks where it had all begun. And in a slow deliberate motion, he took her over and over, letting all the emotions of his age, her beauty, the Brazilian rhythms in the music he had picked, and the short span of this night pour out of him and into her. Into her eyes, her liquid cunt, her stretched ass. Into her soul, and her past. For there was no future. She could tell.

This would be the last and final time. She sensed it in her bones, in her intuition. She hugged him ever so close after he came in a formidable, lasting tremor of pleasure. They fell asleep interlaced, under the colorful wool-knit blanket.

She woke up when his face found her down below. His tongue was still young and experienced, and though she pushed him away at first, he insisted and said, "No, I like it like that." He tasted her for the last time. Her head went back, her eyes rolled upon themselves. No one ever did it like he did. He tasted her with all the love he could muster. He let his fingers capture her scent, and when she was all spent, he crawled back up to her and kissed her like the wind in the trees and the sea on the beach and life upon life.

He stood up and dressed her up again. Same buttons, different man.

He told her the oath was annulled. The Minotaur had vanished, and as a testament of this, he gave her a spool of wool—like Ariadne. She looked at it. It was made of white wool mixed with thin strings of gold. She should weave a garment with it, he said, a thin scarf perhaps, and wear it on future August full moons, for he also said he was soon leaving this Earth. But he assured her that he could, and he would, look upon her on that very day, every year, for every decade, and it would please him to no end to see the inner light of gold upon her loved body.

She told herself that she was not going to cry. The cycle was done, it was over. She would grow from this, she told herself. Yet it was between a sea of tears that she heard him say, "I bought this hut and the land and the winery when you were seventeen. It has always been under your name, my beautiful princess. It is yours to enjoy and dispose of at your leisure. All the documents are with the local clerk."

He held her hand and kissed it goodbye. "Farewell," he told her. "It's time for me to go." He held her hand to his lips a little longer, and then, just like that, he was gone. She sat on the fur for a long, long time. The candles were still burning, and a deep, comforting glow emanated from the white walls. She saw the reflection of the light in her red toenails, and she smiled. He had commented on them, as he always did. He remembered everything, and she could not bear the idea of forgetting him. She rushed back to the open windows. He was still up there on top of the hill. He seemed to be waiting for her, and when he saw her within the window frame, he waved back with his hand. Waved, and then brought his hand to his face. She understood and smiled. She waved back in turn, and this time he disappeared forever.

She turned back inside and slowly blew out all the candles, as if blowing all future memories away.

On the way back to the hotel she saw that lights were on in the suite. She thought that she could see the moving outline of her husband. Oh, how she loved him at that moment. She needed to feel him. To feel real again. To tell him that all the full moons of her life were his only from now on.

In the hut, he had asked, "Is your husband good to you?"

"Yes," she had said. "As good as a wife can dream of."

"Good," he said. "I like him a lot."

She had no time to reflect upon this, she was running up the stairs faster and faster and jumped into the outstretched arms waiting for her.

There was no rhyme or reason for their passionate embrace. They had both slipped onto the other side of the golden disk and yet they kissed each other with the fervor of new love. They found each other's shoulders and backs and ass and everything in between as they stumbled back drunkenly to the bedroom.

He was surprised when he heard her ask, "Rip the dress off me. Rip it now."

He laughed. He told her she sounded like a rapper. And then with full force and might he separated the panels of linen. Buttons came crashing to the floor. One of them noisily hit the bedside wall. They both looked up and saw at the same time the red brassier hanging, like a territorial flag, from the metal hook.

He grabbed it, and once again it made its way into his pocket. She looked at him for a second, her eyebrows arched up. Quizzical. And then her face melted in a wide laughing smile. "You devil," was all she could muster as she pushed herself onto him and the still warm bed.

There was no talking. He took her with all his might, oblivious to everything else, even to the trickle of sperm that gathered around her ass.

They fell asleep again.

The room was never made that day.

By the following morning they had left.

Epilogue

MIA CAME BACK TO WORK the next morning and finished her shift. She had told the manager that this was going to be her last day. On the way in, she had tried to return the clothes to the older woman, who insisted she keep them all. "They look so perfect on you," she said. They ate grapes facing the fantastic sea, and she said her goodbyes.

The woman reminded her of her recently departed grandmother, and now she was homesick. They cried a little when she finally left.

She went back to change at the end of her shift and found a package in her locker. How it got in there, she never knew, but she opened the brown parcel. In it was her red brassiere, threaded through the metal bracelet of the vintage Rolex Submariner he had worn the previous night and a note that simply read:

> *Form follows function indeed.*
> *You are incredible. Thank you.*

She let the watch hang for a moment from the undone garment. All kinds of thoughts raced through her mind. Then she brought it back to the level of her wrist and slipped the dark-faced watch on. It had a beautiful patina and was lighter than she'd thought. He had adjusted the strap. He had guessed right, it fit her fine. Form did follow.

She left the hotel for good—earphones in, listening at the same time as that other person did, unaware that they were sharing the same song today after having shared the same man yesterday.

THE COUPLE DID NOT RETURN TO THE PROPERTY. His father passed away shortly after that summer. As he went through all the estate papers, he realized that somehow, hidden from everyone, the father had launched his far-reaching business empire by buying the very hotel on the beach.

He never told his wife.

She still drinks the white wine from her own island vineyard.

SLACK WATER

—Slack water is the neutral moment, the temporal moment, when the tide is neither moving up nor down.

I T WAS HAPPENING RIGHT OUTSIDE HIS HOME. He did not know. He did not even know the word. He was busy building a fire.

It was a building of sorts. He did as he had seen his father do a long time ago, and he himself must have learned it in the army. He took the old dried-up newspapers that were stored by the fireplace and crumpled them into tight balls. Those would be the initial foundation. Sometimes the headlines from months before would catch his eyes. Old news that appeared ancient. *The Dow Jones Crashes*, said one. He smiled. That was about a year earlier. He'd done well in that crash. Very well, actually. He was renting the house close to the beach now. He liked it enough that he might want to buy it. Most likely it would be for sale. Not everybody had done well in the crash. On top of the coiled newspaper, he laid some wood from a tree the gardener had taken down a while ago. He lit the paper and watched the fire take life. The whole pit was suddenly ablaze with tall flames.

They reminded him of his wife's hair the night before, when he watched her kneel between his legs. Long strands of hair that seemed to have a life of their own. They just sprouted out of her head, like the flames did from the paper.

Next, he put the heavy dry logs on the reddening twigs. But then, nothing much happened. The fire just started to smolder. The flames disappeared.

He went to the garden shed and found the lighter fluid. "Are you starting a fire?" said Milena when he came back in. There was a hint of condescendence in her voice.

"Yes," he replied, squeezing gelatinous fluid over the dying embers. The bottle made a noise, as the fluid squirted out, and then the flames roared up with yet another sound. The room filled up with the smell of burning wood. She liked that.

He had eyes only for her. She was wearing a semi-transparent negligée over what appeared to be her almost naked body. *Negligée* incidentally comes from a French word, which means "neglected." She'd left the top open a little more than necessary, giving him a full view of her beautiful breasts. It did not matter to him that they were fake. They looked fantastic cupped in a lacy black bra.

She had asked for them early on in their courtship. He had initially asked about her favorite jeweler, hinting that he wanted to buy her something. And she had casually said, "I love the idea of jewelry, Sam, but why not pay for my breast implants instead? We'll both benefit from it!" It had been so unexpected and direct, like a transaction. He'd agreed. On the day of the procedure, she got the jewelry as well.

2

HE REALLY WAS QUITE GENTLE WITH HER. At work though, on Wall Street, he was ruthless, and he had the respect of his peers for his determination and sense of overall vision. He loved his job. He spoke about it constantly to her. She thought it was interesting, but not fascinating. Just like their sex life.

She had married him for many reasons. Sex did not top the list. He had other qualities that seemed more important to a thirty-six-year-old woman—his brains, his financial success, his desire to start a family, and his fit physique. She never quite liked his scent though, even when she tried. That was why she liked the fire and the smell of smoke. It overlapped with his scent. She knew what to do. Her mother was Russian, and they know what to do.

He knew deep in him that, although she always seemed

to cum when they were joined, something was not quite right once they got under the covers. He could feel it. It bruised his ego. She was not moving her hips with the passion he so wanted her to feel. She was not always wet enough. She did put on a good act, but it just wasn't there, and he knew it. And he knew that she knew that he knew.

They never spoke about it. Every night he came prepared. He had pills and concoctions in tow, and sometimes toys. She let him go at it, but it remained very vanilla. A necessary convergence if she were to become pregnant. She was doing everything she could to make him cum as often as possible, hence the negligée that day, and the black bra. He realized that the sex they had together was average. That could have satisfied him, but he really loved his wife, which is why it affected him. He wanted to be better for her.

He and Milena had been together for over a year by then, and he was getting slightly desperate. He also wanted children, and he was a firm believer that the moment of conception is primordial. Somewhere deep in him, he felt that it was important that the woman experience the ecstasy of orgasm as the spark of life settled in her. That spark would then go on to light the path of her child.

He was idle in the big house in the Hamptons, golfing only once a week with his brother, who already had two kids. He was falling behind, and he knew it.

He knew she had had another boyfriend shortly before he

met her, and that he'd had sex with her and videotaped them doing it as well. He knew it because she'd inadvertently told him early in their relationship, when she had just enough vodka to make her tipsy and vulnerable. The ex-boyfriend's name was Otto.

Sam had logged onto the computer he had given her as a gift. He opened her contact list and looked for his email address. He was listed under "O" for Otto. Not hidden under a different name. Just Otto. Same as he remembered. Austrian, he believed she had told him before. Otto, the artist. Otto, the one who filmed his wife having sex.

He emailed him using his wife's address and signature. He must have been convincing, for the same afternoon he received the homemade movies. He quickly transferred them to his account and erased all traces of the activity.

He could not wait to open the files, but he wanted to make the moment special. How often do you discover your wife's body seen and taken by another person? He was both excited and apprehensive at the same time. He decided to go to the basement media room to watch on his laptop, somewhere in the corner, deep in the softest of chairs. Like being in business class, he always thought when he sat in one of those seats. Today it may be turbulent.

It certainly had been serious turbulence, right from the beginning. He'd been startled. Her skin was white as snow, and she smiled at the camera with an avidity he had never seen.

But what really struck him at first sight was the fact that she was tied down to the bed. Arms above her, each to a side. Her legs spread wide apart, bound and held open. And despite what appeared like firm restraints, she was smiling widely at the camera.

He focused on her lips, because she was blindfolded. The camera essentially danced across her body with the fluidity of someone who knew what they were looking for—guiding the viewer's eye, like brushstrokes on her eager body, focusing at times on the redness on and in her skin. The camera rolled on. He saw the belt come from behind the field of view and slap her repeatedly. He saw it all. He was mesmerized. Here was his wife, tied up and being slapped with passion and desire. And yet smiling in what appeared to be a continuous orgasm.

He also saw the fake breasts.

This was his slack water moment. Everything could move in one direction or the other.

He was still gasping for air. He had to take control of himself. He looked at it again. Oh, it was her all right, showing more joy on this one clip than in all their nights together: his beautiful, loving, and doting wife caught on film doing the most unexpected things, almost like a plundering.

He could either confront her and carry with him all the cargo of his jealousy, or he could find another solution. He told himself he would wait.

That same night he tried slapping her with the back of his

hand as he hovered above her. It was all out of sync. It hurt without giving pleasure. She realized it in an instant, and she looked at him quizzically. "Baby, are you alright?" she asked.

"Yes, yes. I. . .I just thought that you'd like it."

"Come on, let's sleep," she told him. "It's late already."

He felt terrible. He could not *hit* her. He wasn't made of that cloth.

Yet. . .he watched and re-watched the video clip. He couldn't tell if it was to watch the belt land on her ass at first and then her new breasts a little later. Or if it was to see her contented smile.

That was where he wanted to be, though—right there on that screen, watching and doing. He made himself cum and then went back to bed where she was already sleeping. She looked like an angel, her hair draped around the pillow, her head turned, and with the shadow of his smile on her lips. She was his angel.

He could not believe it yet—everything, the abuse. The timing after the implants were in place.

THE HOT TAP WATER WOULD DISSOLVE all the remains of breakfast. She would watch the yellow of the eggs melt away under the stream, and with it whatever was left of the egg disappeared.

He watched her with new eyes. She still had no idea, no clue about the video.

It was meant to be a day full of simple pleasures that made sense if you appreciated them for their true merit. Simple things, and the lack of something bad or terrible. She turned her head toward him. He was watching her. She could learn to really love him, she thought. Maybe one day after they had a child.

He was wondering, Who was this woman? Who was she *really?* He loved her. He knew that, and he wanted her to love him fully. How could it be if he was not satisfying her deepest desires? Her pleasure was his reward. He dipped his toasted bread into the soft-boiled egg. The yolk offered no resistance. Soon it was the end of that egg as well. Right there and then, he made a plan.

That evening, they drank a little more tequila than usual. Neither of them was a big drinker, and the alcohol, which came in thick, translucent tumblers, transported them to a land of gentle bliss. She could feel his energy, his desire—the way he looked at her, the slight edge in his speech, the way he touched her every time he went past. She liked it. She liked being desired. It was the most potent aphrodisiac, that feeling of being wanted. She fed on it. She looked at him as he was busying himself at nothing tasks, coming back to her and filling her glass again. He smiled at her, even looked at her strangely. She was intrigued, and she drank along—drank the tequila, and drank in his exhilaration.

She was not shocked when he asked her to come with him

to the bedroom. He had a surprise, he said. Such a magical word, *surprise*. She went up to the bedroom and sat at the edge of the large bed. She was looking out at the ocean. It was still visible in the late-summer hour, a dark blue moving line above the trees.

He blindfolded her then, and the ocean disappeared. He asked her to take her clothes off. This startled her. He was not the type to invent and play. He was all business, all the time.

She went along, though, taking off the black Prada shirt, then the cream-colored slacks. She had on a black bra, very thin. It adorned rather than supported her. And a black thong. She always had good underwear on, for herself mainly. Sam never really seemed to care much. She liked putting them on and looking at herself in the mirror. A beautiful body in a beautiful house. Sometimes, that was all it took to make her happy. She waited for a bit. He turned up the music. It was fine. She knew the playlist. He always played the same one.

He pushed her down on the bed, kept the bra on her, pulled off her panties and then, much to her surprise, he tied her hands up in a V. The blindfold was pretty tight. She was in darkness, and now she was tied up. But it was Sam, so she was not worried. He was gentle with her, always. Too gentle. This was a change. She remembered his attempt at slapping her the night before. She wondered what had gone through his mind.

Once he had seen the video, even if he'd tried, he could not un-see it. It was branded in his brain. And what surfaced every time was not her being tied up or receiving the lashes. It was her smile, a smile of pure simple ecstasy he had never personally seen on her face.

That is why he had called Otto, the ex-boyfriend, and asked him to come to the house. He explained what he himself intended to do and what he wanted Otto to do. The young man appeared hesitant. "You're an artist, aren't you?" asked Sam.

"Yes, I am."

"So look at it as if it's a performance. An art performance, for which I will pay six months' rent of your studio."

The answer did not take long to arrive.

He had asked Otto to come unperfumed. And then he sprayed him with his own cologne. He had asked him how to do the knots in order to tie Milena up and he had asked what else he should get. They both picked the belt together from the large walk-in closet. The artist stayed there while Sam got her ready and blindfolded and tied. By the time Otto walked into the room, she was naked except for the black bra. It looked like the wrapping of an expensive gift.

The first thing he did was to dim the lights. He had no shoes, and on the thick wall-to-wall carpet he was silent. He was still silent when he leaned forward and took immense pleasure in smelling her all over again. She had the scent of wealth and luxury he remembered so well. The heavy oriental perfume mixed with her clear skin like colors on his palette. He let the scent fill him up. He could not resist, and he started licking her between her legs, right there in front of Sam. That was not part of the plan. But then again, the landlord had already been paid, and Sam could not make a sound since he was supposed to be alone with Milena.

She was already excited about the blindfold and the tied hands, but she became ecstatic when Sam, or so she still thought, kissed her down below. He never did it, or rarely. She could not remember the last time, and she surely did not remember him being so good at it. Maybe this was a new Sam. In appreciation, she started to moan.

She moaned in a way Sam had never heard her moan before. He was so rattled that he almost forgot to videotape the whole thing. But he did. He felt like a total voyeur recording amateur porn. He decided to keep his eye on the camera screen only. It made everything seem surreal and much easier to cope with. He saw the artist put his fingers up his wife's cunt. And all he could think about was how to get the perfect angle in order to record it all. He watched her being tied up further, her legs spread open. In no time, the belt came down on her. First, a little tap to indicate where the next lash would land, and then *snap!* It actually made more noise than it hurt, but it stung—and she never knew how strong the next lash would be.

He stopped and made her smell his fingers. She breathed herself in as deeply as she could. In doing so, she also had a whiff of the perfume. It was Sam's, but it felt different. It was not hiding an underlying fragrance. It smelled good, as it did when she smelled it from the bottle in the store, before she offered it to her husband. She was surprised. She was perplexed, but she was enjoying herself so much that night that she did not think, and she quickly turned her attention to her legs. He was slapping her hard now, and the blows were inching closer to her pussy. Would he? she thought. No way, she thought. He would never think of injuring her.

Slam!

Without warning, it had landed right between her legs. She squirmed.

Slam! again.

And again—just hard enough to feel it, yet not so hard that it would bruise her.

His fingers were once again in her. She was pouring out juices, she could feel it. And then she tasted it as he put the same fingers in her mouth. The artist looked up at Sam. That was his clue. The real Sam would finish her, would take her, and fuck her, and the artist would leave very quietly, never to be seen again.

Outside the seagulls were flying on the last light, over the last visible waves. You could measure time, measure breath, in the rhythm of these waves.

3

FOR A MOMENT, SAM THOUGHT he should go for a swim in those big Atlantic waves. Cold and firm. Perhaps it would clean all of it. He kept looking at the digital screen and the face of the artist. Two fingers in Milena's mouth, and a quizzical gaze on his own face.

When Sam first received the video, he could have pretended the whole thing had never happened, or he could have been jealous, or he could have tried to learn from it. Even though the fake breasts clearly showed the event had occurred after he met Milena, he decided it must have been her last hurrah. He did not think of her as unfaithful, so he had called the ex-boyfriend and hoped to learn from him. Learn how to please his wife. He had filmed it all—the strap of the belt as it landed on her, the sounds it made, the red marks left on her pale skin, the sound of pleasured moans that poured out of her, streaming from her like the juices between her legs. He had watched it all.

Was he ready to take over?

Seconds were flowing through the room. He could feel them. They were like the waves outside. The moon was high in the sky now and its silver light came through the large bay windows. He watched Milena as she sucked Otto's fingers. The seconds were going faster for her. She loved to feel the hard fingers in her mouth. They tasted of her, and it felt like a cock as well, and she wanted that in her mouth.

Otto looked at Sam one more time. There is a rhythm to great sex, and he knew he had to do something soon.

Sam did not move. He was partially hidden by the camera.

Otto brought his other hand between her legs. She moaned even harder—a long, deep sound that seemed to emanate from a hidden instrument within her. That made things easy for Otto. In one move, he untied one leg and took his pants off, revealing his desire. He kneeled between her legs, licked her some more, and finally went into her with the full thrust of his girth. He danced on her loins, his ass rising and falling towards her, fast and faster.

Milena did not know what to think. Sam had never been quite like that, but now she wasn't sure. She was tied up and could not touch his body. Blindfolded and could not see him. And far enough away that she could neither taste him nor smell him.

She was living a continuous orgasm, one that rippled on and on, and she was not ready to leave that boat. Sam had blindfolded her and tied her up. This was all Sam's doing. She let it happen, willingly opening her body to all the gods of love.

At this point, Sam still had another choice to make. His early indecision had prompted Otto to take over. He understood that. It was a law of business. Either you are at the table, or you are the meal.

Truth be told, he realized that he enjoyed watching. He had never known that about himself. He watched the way Otto kept his wife open with one hand, leaning his weight against her. He filmed it, which made it all the more worthwhile, as if the camera was the validation of the adventure. Now, he had a few choices to make. Any one of them could change their lives forever.

He could go up to her and place his already engorged cock in her mouth, and then she would realize what was happening. She'd realize that there were two men, and that the one in her mouth was Sam. Then he could decide to either remove her blindfold and reveal Otto, with all its consequences, or keep her in the dark, in all manner of speech.

He could also do none of these things. He could wait for Otto to finish, have him leave and lie next to her, holding her tight, and within minutes take her again as if he had a second wind.

Otto was using the belt again, straddling her and slapping her with all the love a lash can bring. He had brought the fabric of her bra down, the big nipples smiling at him. With his hand, he tortured and squeezed them, while slapping her inner thighs and her ass with the belt. He was all over her, hungry for her, for he had loved her at one time, or at least the image of her. And now he could exert vengeance and care all at once, punishing her for having gone safe and comfortable with Sam. Loving her for the fullness of her body, the sweat that pearled on her chest. He slapped her and fucked her until her moans started to overwhelm the crushing waves. He got harder.

That is what that sound is for, to get men even bigger and to make them take you even harder. The sound had a primal pitch—an ancient sound lodged deep in each woman. She released it, louder and louder. After all, they were alone. Sam and she, in the big house. And her hips met his and he came, quickly getting out and spraying her belly and breast. Semen droplets linking themselves to the stretched black silk fabric of her bra. Soon after, Otto was gone. Fast as a cat. His clothes in one hand and shoes in the other.

Sam never contacted him again. That night, Milena got pregnant.

ACKNOWLEDGMENTS

Big thanks to Anouk, Gabrielle, Hugh, Rachel, Renée, Gabriel, and Scott. And special thanks to Kite and Barry.

www.ingramcontent.com/pod-product-compliance
Lightning Source LLC
Chambersburg PA
CBHW041752010726
47507CB00009B/365